**Kurt fought with t̶̶̶̶̶̶̶̶̶̶̶̶̶̶
their truck lurched ̶̶̶̶̶̶̶̶̶̶̶̶̶̶**

The sound of crunching metal filled the cab. The Hummer gave a final shove, and their pickup flipped over the rail. He and Rebecca hung like rag dolls against the seat belts as they vaulted toward the unforgiving water below.

"Protect your head!" he shouted.

The front end slapped into the water, and the truck flipped to the side. Pain blinded Kurt. The sound of rushing water filled the back seat.

"Kurt! Kurt, are you okay? Should I open the door? Roll down the window?" Rebecca's questions came out as fast cries that he could barely comprehend. They hung upside down with all the windows and doors covered in water. The doors wouldn't budge until they stopped sinking and reached equilibrium. The statistics of water crashes had been drilled in his head. They had thirty, maybe ninety seconds at the most before they lost any chance of survival...

Heather Woodhaven earned her pilot's license, rode a hot-air balloon over the safari lands of Kenya, parasailed over Caribbean seas, lived through an accidental detour onto a black-diamond ski trail in Aspen and snorkeled among stingrays before becoming a mother of three and wife of one. She channels her love for adventure into writing characters who find themselves in extraordinary circumstances.

Books by Heather Woodhaven

Love Inspired Suspense

CREDIBLE THREAT

HEATHER WOODHAVEN

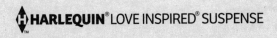

If you purchased this book without a cover you should be aware that this book is stolen property. It was reported as "unsold and destroyed" to the publisher, and neither the author nor the publisher has received any payment for this "stripped book."

Recycling programs
for this product may
not exist in your area.

LOVE INSPIRED BOOKS

ISBN-13: 978-1-335-49019-3

Credible Threat

Copyright © 2018 by Heather Humrichouse

All rights reserved. Except for use in any review, the reproduction or utilization of this work in whole or in part in any form by any electronic, mechanical or other means, now known or hereinafter invented, including xerography, photocopying and recording, or in any information storage or retrieval system, is forbidden without the written permission of the editorial office, Love Inspired Books, 195 Broadway, New York, NY 10007 U.S.A.

This is a work of fiction. Names, characters, places and incidents are either the product of the author's imagination or are used fictitiously, and any resemblance to actual persons, living or dead, business establishments, events or locales is entirely coincidental.

This edition published by arrangement with Love Inspired Books.

® and TM are trademarks of Love Inspired Books, used under license. Trademarks indicated with ® are registered in the United States Patent and Trademark Office, the Canadian Intellectual Property Office and in other countries.

www.Harlequin.com

Printed in U.S.A.

And whatsoever ye do, do it heartily, as to the Lord, and not unto men.

–Colossians 3:23

To the fire marshal who thought my research questions were grounds for placing me on the FBI watch list, thank you for still talking to me. Also, if it makes you feel better, I'm pretty sure my search history placed me on that list seven books ago.

ONE

Rebecca Linn slid in her socks across the gleaming wood floor, cozy and happy to be in her favorite flannel pajamas. She filled the ceramic mug with hot water and a chamomile tea bag before returning to her grandfather's desk. She had one more week in Coeur D'Alene, Idaho, to finish up an audit for Vista Resort Properties before flying back to Ohio.

Her firm would've put her up in the resort and spa, but it seemed like a conflict of interest to audit the company while being pampered in one of their resorts. Besides, her grandfather, a federal judge in town, owned a magnificent house overlooking the lake. Staying at his place was luxurious enough.

She dropped into the desk chair and her empty laptop bag fell to the ground. A black flash drive slipped out of the front pocket, reflecting off the soft glow of the desk lamp. Rebecca leaned forward and squinted. She'd never seen it before and she'd just reorganized her bag that morning before meeting with the accountants of Vista Resorts. She picked up the drive and turned it in her fingers. Other than a scratch on the back, the casing had no telltale markings to jog her memory.

Babette, a Siamese mix with white fur and blue eyes, jumped onto the ornate cherry desk and flopped down onto her side beside Rebecca's laptop, purring. She absently moved to pet her with one hand, but the cat swatted her away. Figured. She liked only Grandpa. "What are we going to do about this, Babette?"

The cat held up her head for a second but didn't answer. Procedure would have her send the strange drive into the corporate office for the IT department to scan, but it wasn't as if she'd found it in the middle of a parking lot. It had been in her laptop bag. So, either one of the accountants had accidentally placed it in her bag or one of them had put it there on purpose.

A few hours earlier an accountant had bumped into her on his way out of the building. There had been plenty of room in the hallway—in fact she'd been standing to the side, admiring the potted plants that resembled mini palm trees—so she knew it'd been on purpose. She'd waited for him to try to hit on her but instead he'd rushed out the front door without so much as an apology. What if she had a whistle-blower on her hands? In that scenario, it seemed more prudent to see what was on the drive than to wait for a few days for IT to sort it out. Sleep wouldn't come any time soon without satisfying her curiosity.

She turned off all internet access and inserted the stick into the USB port of her laptop. The chamomile tea had cooled enough to sip on while she waited for the antivirus software to scan the contents. Finally the cursor reappeared and allowed her to click on the lone file.

A spreadsheet of Vista Resorts' assets and liabilities, remarkably similar to the one she'd saved on her online server, loaded. She never would've put a client's information on a portable, unrecognizable drive, so that definitely ruled out any forgetful actions on her part. As she scrolled down the spreadsheet, several lines were highlighted in yellow.

"What are we looking at?" she muttered to Babette. It seemed that millions of dollars had been diverted to—

A creak behind her sent chills up her spine. The intrigue of the mysterious flash drive coupled with the settling of the house had turned her nerves to jelly.

Babette perked her ears and sat up in attention. That was odd. The cat let out a warbled growl that should've made her laugh if she wasn't so freaked out. She spun around to the empty living room. The open floor plan allowed her to see the kitchen, as well, from her vantage point.

Rebecca blew out a breath. "See, it was nothing." She grabbed her phone anyway. In reality, she had nothing to fear. Her grandfather owned a state-of-the-art security system and he'd made a point to tell her it was activated before he'd left. No alarm meant there was nothing to worry about. Her fingers clutched the phone tighter despite the reassuring thoughts.

The cat released another growl. Perhaps an early spring fly had flown into the house. Babette loved to hunt.

Rebecca walked toward the kitchen. Maybe the ice maker had caused the creak. The open layout allowed her to walk into the next room without any doors. She peered out of the ceiling-to-floor window, straining to see outside. Aside from the reflection of the moon off the lake, nothing seemed out of the ordinary.

The darkness of the hill changed, as if in motion. She blinked and could see only the reflection of the furniture in the living room—and a man in a ski mask rushing toward her.

A scream tore from her throat and her chest seized in panic. She launched to the side, toward the back door. An arm snaked around her torso as a hand clasped over her mouth in such a swift motion that her phone flew out of her hand and hit the floor.

He pulled against her middle and dragged her backward across the floor. Rebecca squirmed and writhed against his steel arms to no avail. She tried to suck in a breath, but his hand covered her nose, as well.

Scratchy material brushed up against her cheek. "You're coming with me either way." He didn't bother to whisper. So he knew they were all alone in the house. "It's up to you whether you're injured along the way."

He moved just enough that air slipped through his fingers. She inhaled, but his heavy, spiced breath turned her stomach. There was no way a masked man trying to force her out of the house would earn her trust. If he got her into a car, she knew the statistics of survival wouldn't be in her favor.

An oval mirror hanging on the wall opposite the desk in the living room showed her struggle. Her hazel eyes bulged against her taut, pale face, and the man's lips formed a snarl over bared teeth surrounded by the black fabric of the mask. The visual image simultaneously horrified and cleared her mind.

She flung her legs out in a wide squat and dropped

her weight like she'd seen her toddler nephew do a dozen times. The man grunted at the sudden change. His left arm pressed against her ribs so hard she cried out. He yanked her back again, but she sunk into her squat and he managed only to slide her another foot.

Rebecca twisted her hips to get her right foot behind the man's left leg. She shoved her knee into the back of his leg in the hope it'd throw him off balance, but he didn't budge. She bent her torso over fast, and his hand slid off her mouth for half a second before he yanked her hair instead. She screamed at the ripping sensation of her scalp, but as her chin lifted she saw a patch of exposed skin.

Her hand curled into a fist and she punched his neck. He gagged and released her long enough for her to elbow him in the stomach.

The cat screeched and the man bellowed. Rebecca didn't look up long enough to see what the cat had done. She grabbed the shiny gold letter opener on the desk with her left hand and spun around, not even watching where she was going. The sharp edge slit across his arm and stomach. He jumped back with a roar.

"Get back!" She gripped the opener with her entire fist and shook it at him. His dark eyes watched her. He seemed more angry than hurt, with an air of confidence that he could overtake her again if he wanted. She didn't wait to find out.

She bolted for the front door, an unbidden screech tearing from her lips. The front door had been left ajar. She slapped the panic button with her free hand as she flung the door fully open with her left shoulder.

She sprinted down the long driveway, listening

for the slap of feet behind her. Silence only followed. The panic alarm never sounded. In fact, the alarm should've gone off when the intruder had entered.

Hidden in between the two evergreen trees in the yard was a black SUV-shaped vehicle. She flinched and ran to the far edge of the driveway, wondering if another attacker sat inside the vehicle. No headlights or engine sounds greeted her. The license plate on the vehicle was too dark to see, and there was no way she was going to investigate.

Her instinct demanded she yell "fire," although she couldn't remember why, only that she'd been taught to do so if in danger. "Fire!" she yelled so hard it stung her throat. She shouted repeatedly and ran down the quarter-mile drive to the main road. No one came to her aid.

Her feet stung from the loose chips of asphalt pressing into the thin layer of her socks. Her grandfather had no close neighbors. The lot sat on a two-acre hill overlooking the lake. She rounded the corner and ran into the street.

She chanced a glance over her shoulder but didn't see anyone following her. Her attacker had worn all black. Or was she remembering correctly? It all happened so fast. It was possible he was out there, following her, watching her, waiting to pounce. That beast of a vehicle could suddenly come to life in a heartbeat.

She screamed for help, as if on a repeating loop, while she ran down the road. Her head swiveled constantly, searching for safety and possible threats. Headlights rounded the curve. She rushed toward them, flailing her arms.

At the last second, she realized it looked like she

was waving a knife. She flung the letter opener to the side of the road and clasped her hands in front of her chest, pleading for help. The car didn't so much as slow as it bared down on her.

Please, Lord.

It kept coming. The bumper barreled toward her. The headlights blinded her and she jumped out of the way. Pain rushed up her leg as gravel at the side of the road shifted underneath her toes.

Her balance lost, her fingers reached to grasp for something but met only air as she fell backward into the ditch.

Deputy United States Marshal Kurt Brock lengthened his stride down the hospital hallway. The smell of antiseptic burned the back of his throat. Tension in the back of his neck begged for some time in his massage chair at home, but time didn't allow it.

He had made it home at midnight, after a successful capture of a fugitive in Montana, only to be beckoned by a federal judge at five in the morning. Hopefully the visit would be quick and he could go back to a much-needed couple days off. While he didn't work for the judges, he served them. When a federal judge had a need, the Marshals jumped to try to accommodate.

He stepped in front of a closed hospital door where his coworker, Deputy Delaney Patton, stood guard. Kurt nodded and straightened his tie. They didn't know each other well enough to chitchat—not that he was one to shoot the breeze—as their paths didn't cross very often. Kurt usually worked alone. He lifted his chin and searched for any sign of the stocky judge.

"The judge went to the cafeteria to get coffee." Del-

aney shook her head, the light brown hair from her po-
nytail swishing in an arc. "He won't let anyone take
a statement from her but you. Word from the boss is
he wants you to lead the investigation. I'm to assist in
any way you see fit. She's ready to bolt, so the sooner
you talk to her the better." Delaney stepped to the side.

Kurt inhaled. Without a full briefing, all he knew
was that the judge's granddaughter had barely escaped
a kidnapping attempt. He steeled himself for the worst.
Seeing a child hurt was the worst part of his job. He
pressed the swinging door. "US Marshals. May I come
in?" he asked softly.

"Yes," a soft, sweet voice replied.

He stepped past a curtain and felt his eyes widen
as he stared at the gorgeous woman before him. This
was no child.

She pulled her chin inward at the sight of him. She
worried her lip and pulled up the hospital sheet with
one hand. Her other hand brushed her curly brown
hair, marred only by an oddly positioned gauze head-
band of sorts, away from her face.

Kurt realized his surprise at her appearance had
likely caused the self-conscious actions. "I don't mean
to stare."

"It's okay. I know I must be a sight."

"No, no, you look…uh—" He exhaled loudly. Sleep
usually helped with foot-in-mouth disease and he was
sorely lacking. He needed to start over and hope the
deputy outside hadn't heard his social blunder. "When
I heard Judge Linn's granddaughter was here, I expected someone younger. I've never come right out and
asked the judge's age—" Oh, great. First the granddaughter thought he was appalled by her appearance

and now it sounded like he had opinions about how soon the judge had started having kids.

Her eyebrows rose before she nodded, a small laugh escaping. "He's eighty-six. He's almost got sixty years on me." Her fingers rolled the edge of the blanket like a scroll.

"Judge Linn looks young for his age, then." Kurt hoped that cleared the air so he could begin again. Over 10 percent of the sitting judges were in their eighties, but Judge Linn had more drive and passion than most sixty-year-olds. "Are you up for talking about what happened?"

She dropped the sheet from her fingertips. "Oh, yes." She gingerly touched the gauze underneath her hair. "I could've gone home last night, according to one of the nurses, but Grandpa insisted the doctors keep me overnight as a precaution." She eyed him as if trying to decide whether to trust him. "When Grandpa wants something, he usually gets it, so I didn't argue."

Kurt ignored that potential minefield. "Concussion?"

"Maybe. I didn't pay much attention to what the doctor said after the events of the night. I...uh...kept trying to remember more. Identifying factors." She turned her attention to the window. "The headache wasn't much fun, either, but that's gone away. Just a little stiff and sore." She let her head sink back into the stack of pillows behind her. "I hit a rock near the base of my neck. Thankfully my muscles and skull took most of the impact instead of my spine."

He'd had enough similar close calls to know the pain and stiffness had to be intense. "My understanding is someone almost ran you over when you tried to get help."

She sucked in a deep breath and nodded. "A teenager. He said he didn't see me until it was almost too late, but he waited with me in the ditch until the police came."

The driver probably didn't want to admit that he had been on his cell phone while driving. Kurt held back his frustration but hoped the cops who'd arrived on the scene had scared the kid enough with scenarios of what could've happened that the boy would never text and drive again. "And the attacker?"

She shook her head. "No sign. The police didn't find him."

Delaney walked inside the room from her spot at the door. "I received confirmation that the assailant turned off the security cameras at the front patio, so we don't have any footage."

Kurt's heart rate increased as he thought about the judge's house. "He bypassed the security system?"

"No alarm. The panic button did nothing," Rebecca answered.

He knew the security system well. Top-of-the-line wireless security system with cellular backup. He'd approved it last year with the chief deputy's blessing before it was installed. They liked to keep systems up-to-date and replaced them at regular intervals. The kidnapping attempt was alarming by itself, but knowing how to disarm technology like that wasn't normal for a run-of-the-mill criminal. He schooled his features as if it was an everyday occurrence. He didn't need to upset her further. "Okay. Anything you can tell me about your attacker? Any recognizable features?"

"He was in a mask. A black ski mask. He wore…" She licked her lips and looked up at the ceiling tiles as she blinked rapidly. "I can't remember."

Shame filled her voice; an understandable sentiment but unnecessary. Victims often had a tough time remembering those details. "Don't beat yourself up or try to push it. It's been hours, you've had a bump on your head and—"

"I'd recognize his eyes and his voice. I'm sure of it. He had a unique accent."

"Do you know what kind?"

She shook her head. "Foreign. Not European. Someone who spoke Spanish but more of the Latin variety." She shrugged. "I know it's not very helpful, but it's all—"

"You're doing great. What exactly did he say to you?"

The door to the room swung inward and Justice Linn strode past Delaney and Kurt with two cups of coffee in his hands. He wore a colorful sweater that reminded Kurt of the early nineties, tan slacks and matching loafers. His hair, while thinning on top, was a blend of brown and gray that looked natural.

It was no wonder Kurt thought he was younger. He nodded at the judge. "Chief Justice Li—"

"Brock, it's about time you showed up." His forceful tone would make a less confident man feel nervous. The judge didn't make eye contact, but handed his granddaughter the cup. "Here you go, sweetie." He spun around. "I requested you. I want someone with experience on this, and I want it dealt with immediately."

Since they had only two deputy marshals stationed

in the Coeur D'Alene office, and Delaney was a newbie fresh out of basic training, it seemed a reasonable request. Kurt hoped Delaney didn't take it as a slight against her. "Sir, I'm afraid I haven't finished interview—"

"Someone attempted to kidnap my granddaughter last night." The judge's bloodshot eyes scanned the room as his lower lip quivered. "There's no question about it. I want this treated as a direct threat to the court." He pointed his index finger at the ground as if physically punctuating the sentence.

The truth was that it was highly probable the threat was aimed at him. Judge Linn had served for almost forty years, mostly in the criminal court. All judges received threats, but the number had risen exponentially over the past decade. Many of those threats were specifically aimed at family members, though usually it was immediate family. "Sir, have you or Rebecca spoken about this with the police?"

"They're ill equipped," Judge Linn answered. "You need to take over."

Kurt appreciated the man's faith in him, but they were going to need to work hand in hand with the police. He gestured toward the door, where Delaney waited. "I was told that Miss Linn lives in Ohio." Of course, when his boss had told him, he'd imagined her as a little girl whose parents were waiting back in Cincinnati, not a grown woman. "We could escort her to the airport once she's discharged. We'll continue investigating the threat from this end."

Judge Linn's frown intimidated him more than any other superior officers did. "She's staying here." He turned back to Rebecca and his features softened. "Though I wish you'd change your mind. I know why

you're doing this. Don't pretend you're not staying
for me."

Kurt marveled at the change in tenor when the
judge spoke to his granddaughter. He didn't understand all the undertones of their hushed conversation,
but it seemed like the judge didn't want to admit he'd
rather have her back in Ohio, as well.

She beamed. "No one is scaring me away. You
know I have a job to finish here before I can go. Besides, I can help them identify the man. I would recognize his voice and his eyes anywhere. Plus, I hurt
him." Rebecca tilted her head so she could address
Kurt around her grandfather. "He should have a cut
along his arm or…" She closed her eyes and held up
her right fist as if reliving it. "His right shoulder, to
be more precise. I cut him with a letter opener." She
exhaled and looked past the judge. "I think I at least
scratched his chest, as well."

Kurt didn't want to admit aloud that he was impressed, but she would be an asset in catching the attacker quickly. "If you drew blood, we could run a
DNA test off the letter opener."

She cringed. "It's somewhere on the side of the
road. Near the ditch I fell in."

"Delaney, please have some officers sent to locate
the evidence." He tried to keep his jaw from clench-
ing. If the police had interviewed her last night, they
could've nabbed the guy by now.

Delaney spun on her heel and rushed out of the
room.

"I don't want this in the papers, Brock," Judge Linn
barked. "I need to go to the Boise courts for trial, and
I don't want her fighting a media circus."

All of the federal judges within the state traveled between the three US courts in Idaho. But, if Judge Linn went now, the marshals would need reinforcements to provide for his protective detail. The deputy marshals stationed in Boise had their hands full. Many were out on fugitive cases like the one he just finished. They weren't going to like the news. "Sir, we're going to need police cooperation."

Judge Linn ignored him for a moment as he gently kissed Rebecca's forehead. Her eyelashes fluttered and Kurt found himself wishing he could see her pretty eyes up close.

The judge straightened. "Brock, a word alone."

Kurt may have imagined it, but he thought he saw Rebecca fight a laugh as if she knew he was in for a lecture. He supposed she'd warned him when she'd said her grandpa was used to getting what he wanted.

Kurt stepped into the hallway as the judge rounded on him, finger in the air. "She refuses to go to Ohio because she's scared she'll lead the threat to her father—my son." The judge shook his head. "If he hears a single word of this, he'll never speak to me again. That sweet girl knows it and is determined to stay here until the threat is gone." He narrowed his eyes. "Make sure there is no threat. Understood?"

It wasn't his job to sort out family drama, but Kurt wanted to eliminate the threat as much as he did. "We'll do our best, sir. You have my word."

The judge frowned, nodded and took a step toward the elevator. "Oh…and, Brock?" He held up the same finger in the air but didn't turn to look back. "I'm sure you already know that my granddaughter is beautiful and intelligent."

Kurt's spine stiffened. Unsure of what to say, he simply responded, "Yes, sir."

"Don't feel you need to get to know her any better. You read me?"

In other words, Kurt was to keep his distance. "Loud and clear, sir." He didn't need to be told twice.

All he needed to do was to keep her safe, catch the bad guy and put her on a plane back to Ohio.

TWO

Rebecca wanted nothing more than to turn her thoughts off, but if she stopped obsessing over the attack, she feared she'd forget some crucial detail. As soon as she got back to Grandpa's place, she wanted some time alone on her laptop. Typing every single detail she remembered would allow her to get it off her mind and finally relax. At least, as much as she could unwind with two marshals guarding her.

She pulled her unruly hair back into a loose braid and secured it with a rubber band a nurse offered her. It embarrassed her a little bit to leave the hospital in a business suit, but her grandfather had grabbed the first thing he'd seen from her suitcase. He had already left with a policeman who would meet a deputy marshal from Boise in McCall to take over his protective detail. If her father knew she had been assigned her own protective detail, he'd lose his mind with worry, but she couldn't deal with that yet.

Rebecca stepped out of the bathroom. Kurt faced the door. His thick brown hair was slightly lighter than hers, and she wondered if it was natural or from so much time outside. His skin, slightly tanned, seemed to indicate the latter. He leaned against the wall as he made notes on his tablet. His dress shirt was a bit strained at the center of his back. She knew from the way her brother complained that it was hard to find athletic fits of dress clothes.

The marshal was much bigger, much stronger, than her first glance had led her to believe. Guys like him probably spent all their free time in a gym. She couldn't help but wonder if he would win a one-on-one fight against her attacker. Her attacker hadn't looked as fit or seemed as strong as the marshal, but she shivered at the memory of the cold, calculated way he'd stared at her when she'd screamed for him to get away.

Kurt swiveled. His kind brown eyes searched her face. "Hey, are you okay?" He placed a steadying hand on her arm and his heat was enough to make her forget it was chilly. "You've gone pale. I can call the doctor."

She blinked. "I'm fine. I was lost in thought, wondering why he let me get away."

He stepped back and tilted his head. "Get away?"

She fidgeted with the edge of her suit jacket, curling it—a habit she couldn't seem to break—and fought to ground herself in the present moment. "I'd like to think I got away because I did the right things, but…" She shook her head and cleared her throat. "The more I think about it, he probably could've caught up to me. Why didn't he?"

Kurt crossed his arms over his chest. "Ma'am, you did do the right things. You fought back, you ran and you tried to get help."

"You can call me Rebecca." She turned her attention to the tiled floor. And while she appreciated his comforting words, it didn't diminish her newfound fear. Her job required lots of travel. As a single woman, she took precautions and remained observant, but if she started to jump at her own shadow, she wouldn't be able to cope.

His feet shifted as if uncomfortable. "You've met my fellow marshal, Delaney Patton. She and the police have secured your grandfather's house. I'll take you back there now, if you're ready."

She looked around the room but realized she had no personal effects. If Grandpa hadn't brought her shoes, she wouldn't even have that.

They walked to the elevator and parking lot in silence until they reached a massive white pickup.

He exhaled. "I wasn't expecting…uh… We should have an official sedan available in a day or so. I hope you don't mind riding in this today."

"No, I don't care a bit."

He opened the door for her and offered his hand. She almost refused it except her head still hurt and it was quite a big step up into the seat. The moment her fingers touched his palm, her stomach flipped. He jerked his hand back as if she'd shocked him with static electricity. She elected to use the inside door handle to help her into the cab instead and he kept his sights on their surroundings, constantly swiveling his head until he closed the door behind her.

When she'd first met him, he'd seemed more friendly and approachable, but maybe she'd misjudged. As he slid into the driver's seat she asked, "So have you been a deputy marshal a long time?" He nodded but said nothing.

"Enjoy your work?"

Another nod.

Well, he wasn't going to help her keep her mind off the attack at this rate. She leaned back into the seat as he cranked the car's ignition. Music blared through the speakers. She flinched at the sound of violins feverishly accelerating through the measures.

"Sorry." The marshal swiftly turned down the volume. "I wasn't expecting a passenger."

"What was that?" she asked with emphasis on each word.

"An orchestral arrangement of 'Toccata and Fugue in D Minor' by Bach."

She felt her eyes widen. The idea of a buff marshal driving a beefed-up truck with classical music booming cracked her up. "I didn't mean the song title…" She gestured at the speakers inside the truck.

His lips curved to the side. "You were expecting country?"

"I don't know, maybe." She looked at his profile. "More like hard rock."

He shrugged. "I rock out…to classical music." A small smile crept up and threatened to melt her knees as he glanced at her before backing out of the parking lot. "The instrumental music keeps my head clear. It helps my focus."

He squeezed the steering wheel and frowned as if surprised he'd just admitted as much to her. "We'd better get you to safety." He reached in the back seat with one arm and handed her a ball cap with the Marshals star logo in the center. "Wear this and keep your head down."

The solemn reality of her situation came crashing down. She followed his directions and slouched in the seat. The conversational, encouraging man disappeared once again. Her first impression must've been completely wrong. The man was all business. Until they found her attacker it would be like hanging out with a brick wall. All the more motivation to figure out who the intruder was and to get him behind bars so she could go back to living her life.

Five silent minutes passed before he pulled into Grandpa's driveway. Two police officers on either side of the entrance waved them forward. The garage opened to reveal Delaney inside, standing next to the controls and connecting door. She, at least, offered a welcoming smile.

Rebecca reached for the door handle.

"Stay in the vehicle until the garage is secure," Kurt said. He watched the rearview mirror until they were enclosed.

Delaney walked around the front of the car and opened the passenger door. "I'm sure you're ready to rest," she said.

"Did you find anything off the letter opener?"

"I'm afraid we haven't found it at all yet."

Everything looked different inside the house. All the blinds had been pulled down on the floor-to-ceiling windows. The soothing view of the mountains and the lake had been replaced with a kitchen counter full of walkie-talkies and other contraptions Rebecca didn't recognize.

"I've arranged for the police to take shifts on the perimeter of the property. Judge Linn's assistant has been gathering any cases she thinks worthy of note, aside from our own log of threats." Delaney tapped her phone with each sentence as if checking off a list as she spoke to Kurt.

"How many threats have been made?" Rebecca asked.

Kurt and Delaney both wore the deer-caught-in-the-headlights look, as if they'd forgotten she was in the room. Delaney was the first to snap out of it and held her hand out to Kurt, as if waiting for him to answer. When he looked uncomfortable, she faced Rebecca. "You have to keep in mind that there are over two thousand sitting federal judges. And in any given year we could have anywhere from five hundred to over a thousand threats."

"I'm not asking about the others. How many has my grandfather received during his time as a judge?" Rebecca put her hands on her hips. She knew from auditing hundreds of companies when someone was trying to keep something from her. "Or would it be better that I ask my grandfather directly?" She wanted to help law enforcement remove the threat, but she would not stand to be treated like a frail wallflower.

Kurt faced her but didn't make eye contact. "Almost three hundred."

She lost the ability to breathe for a moment. Three hundred people had threatened to hurt or kill Grandpa or his family? *Her* family? "That's…wow." No wonder her dad wanted to keep her as far away from the judge as possible. He'd made her promise she wouldn't go into law enforcement or be with someone who was.

Maybe she could find some of the threats online. Surely some of them had made the news. Then she could identify the man and wrap it up before dinner. She spun in a circle, looking around the wooden floor for her phone. Hopefully the screen protector had worked as promised.

"I found your phone," Delaney said. "We haven't screened it yet, though, so please avoid using it. Tracey, the officer outside, has agreed to act as a courier until his shift ends. Our computer guy, Mike, will stay late to scan any electronics for spyware as soon as you bag it up. I'll keep you updated."

Rebecca held up her hand in a half-hearted wave but Delaney was already halfway out the door.

"If you don't mind unlocking your phone for me, I need to take a superficial look before we bag it."

Even the timbre of his voice made the back of her neck tingle. She crossed to the counter to pick it up. "Okay. But can I ask why?"

"Precautionary step, and I've been trained to see red flags that might speed up tracking the attacker. After our guy at the courthouse takes care of it, we'll feel confident you can use it. Mike's an expert. You'll have it back in no time. Like the judge, you are accepting our protection detail of your own free will. You don't have to, but I recommend it."

"You don't have to convince me." She tried to smile as she thought about everything on her device. He'd see all of her app choices, like the funny photo manipulation application her niece, Mandy, insisted she try for all the selfies they exchanged. Not to mention the games Mandy begged her to download like Minecraft and Candy Crush. "I've been meaning to delete a few things anyway."

"I understand." His lips shifted to the right as if trying not to laugh at her.

"Maybe I can just do that real quick before—"

He lost the war and laughed. "Rebecca, it'd be better if you let me check first. I'm not here to judge."

It was a glimmer of the man who'd first come in to interview her. Maybe he switched on the no-nonsense persona when in protection mode.

The screen was intact, thankfully. She clicked on the phone to enter her pass code and several previews of text messages from friends and colleagues popped up on the home page. It was nothing that couldn't wait, but it unnerved her. She'd almost been kidnapped… or worse.

Everyone in her life still assumed she was having a blast.

His fingers brushed against hers as she handed him the phone. His eyes darted to meet hers and she looked away. Her laptop still remained open on the desk in the living area, but the black flash drive sat next to it. Odd.

She crossed the room. "Would the other marshal, Delaney, already have checked my computer?"

"I don't believe so. I'll want to do a preliminary scan before we send it in, as well."

"Someone took out the flash drive." She'd had it plugged in when the man had attacked, although there was a possibility it could've been knocked out when she'd grabbed the letter opener.

While Kurt recommended he scan everything first, she'd never sleep without following her hunch. "I have to check something for work before you take this. Feel free to watch for those flags," she said. She sat and inserted the drive back into the USB drive before Kurt could object.

The spreadsheet appeared and she scrolled down. "Unbelievable. Someone wanted me to think it's the same flash drive, but it's not." The highlighted problem areas were nowhere to be found. She examined the file a second time but didn't find anything. Her heart raced and the throbbing headache returned.

She spun around to face the marshal. "What if this isn't about the judge?"

"What makes you think it wouldn't be?" Kurt lowered the phone and placed it on the desk beside the laptop.

"I'm sure that this flash drive was plugged into my computer when I was attacked." She gestured toward a spreadsheet full of hundreds of numbers that made his mind go numb.

"It's possible you misremembered. I'll scan the flash drive for spyware, as well."

"No, it's not that…" She released a frustrated exhale and yanked the drive from the computer. The laptop sounded the obnoxious beep that meant she didn't eject it properly. She flipped the black stick over in her hand, studying it carefully. "It's missing a couple of lines I'm sure were there last night."

"For your job? Do you have it saved elsewhere?"

"Yes, yes I have backups. I'm trying to tell you there was something on this drive last night that's not here today. And I don't have any copies of that. In fact this isn't even my flash drive. It appeared in my bag last night. It might've been put there by a whistle-blower." Her eyes widened and she shoved her finger at the middle of the drive. "I knew it! The drive last night had a scratch on it." She waved the black object in front of him. "This one looks brand-new."

Her eyes looked a little manic. He glanced at the bandage wrapped around her hair. How hard had she hit her head? Rebecca's eyes narrowed and she crossed her arms, as if she already knew what he was about to say. His job required him to say the tough things sometimes, but he knew how to do so tactfully. "Sometimes, after a head injury—"

"I can't believe you went there." She rolled her eyes and leaned back into the chair.

"Listen, even aside from the blow to the head, you were in a dangerous situation last night. Adrenaline and panic can make some details fuzzy." His training included a basic understanding of what victims and witnesses went through. They'd even put his class into a mock crime and asked them to identify the perp by mug shots that were two years old. Most of them had failed. "Don't beat yourself up or push yourself. The best thing—"

She moved her hands in front of her face as if wiping away his words. "You don't have to tell me that. I was there. I vividly remember it all." Her face paled.

Kurt fought the urge to put his hand on her shoulder or to pull her into a hug. He'd never had similar inclinations during other protection assignments. It took him off guard. He stepped backward for more distance.

She pulled her knees to her chest and wrapped her arms around her legs. Wearing her business suit, the action made her look even more vulnerable. "I know I'm not perfect." Her voice was soft and lyrical. "I realize I could remember some details wrong. But about this…" She took a deep breath and stared ahead at a spot on the wall, as if recalling the attack again. "I'm sure," she whispered. "There's no way I imagined it. This is a different drive than the one in my bag."

He closed the laptop and unplugged it. He slipped it, alongside the drive and cell phone, inside a bag that blocked all cellular signals and tracking. He opened the front door and gestured for the officer at the edge of the driveway to come get the bag. He set it down on the concrete for the officer to courier to the courthouse.

"What are you doing?"

He locked the door and faced her. "Don't worry. You'll get it back soon. If there's any chance you are right, the flash drive could've installed spyware on your computer to watch and listen to the judge. As soon as you did it, they would've known, and maybe they wanted to get rid of the evidence and let you go."

"Like a fake out? So I wouldn't suspect they were spying on me? But there were numbers on the drive related to my work."

He studied her a little longer than he needed. "Maybe you should explain your job a little more."

"I work for a global accounting firm. We specialize in third-party audits, mainly for investment purposes. My firm had an audit request here in Coeur D'Alene and, since my grandfather lives here, my boss thought of me for the assignment."

He crossed his arms over his chest. "Then I can put your mind to rest. Typically only IRS auditors get threatened." Her eyes narrowed again, so he humored her. "Who is your audit for?"

"Vista Resort Properties. The corporate offices as well as their biggest resort and spa are located here. The CEO told me a potential investor requested my firm specifically."

He almost laughed. People who specialized in vacations had to have the easiest jobs in the world. The likelihood the threat could be from a resort, of all things, seemed unlikely. If they got upset at someone, all they needed to do was take their own advice and get a massage or rest in a hammock. He'd pay good money for either thing at the moment.

Her hypothesis most likely had more to do with work stress and maybe the head injury. "I know you don't want your family to be in danger, but a company that specializes in relaxing spas is definitely not after you."

A storm seemed to brew in her eyes. "They bring in *millions* of dollars each year. It's not out of the realm of possibility."

Kurt held up his hands in mock surrender. "Okay. I'll add them to the list, but I think we should pool our resources and look at credible threats first. I can access ones made in public with a simple search. If you're up for it, I'd like to see if you recognize anyone while we wait for Delaney to send us more files."

Rebecca blinked rapidly and nodded. "Of course. I'm just going to make some tea while you pull them up." She stood quickly and wobbled. Her hand reached for her forehead.

Kurt instinctively rushed to catch her. He placed his arm around the back of her waist as she leaned into him.

Her cheeks flushed as she focused on the ground. "I'm fine. Just stood up too fast. I think I'm a bit de-hydrated."

Not to mention the aforementioned head injury, but Kurt knew not to bring up that sensitive topic again. His arm lingered a moment longer as she looked up into his eyes. "Thank you." Her voice was soft and gentle to his ears.

Uh-oh. Kurt dropped his arm and strode to the door

leading to the garage. He refused to let his mind wander on how much he enjoyed having her in his arms. "Your blood sugar might be low, too. We can order some food in if you don't have anything to eat here. I'm going to grab my equipment while you make yourself that tea."

He reached his truck and blew out a breath. Talking a lot wasn't his style, yet he'd practically ranted. There was something that drew him to Rebecca. A completely unfair set of feelings, as the judge had practically ordered him to keep his distance. Sure, Judge Linn wasn't his boss, but Kurt also didn't want to make an unnecessary enemy on the court. One recommendation from the judge could go a long way in securing a promotion.

He left his two other weapons stored in the vehicle but grabbed his on-the-go duffel, which contained some of his gear and clothes. Ninety percent of assignments involved tracking down fugitives. He needed his head to get in the game in the same manner, tracking down an unnamed threat.

The protection part of the assignment wouldn't even be an issue as long as she stayed inside the house, so maybe he had a chance to get Rebecca out of his mind. They could go through threats then keep to opposite ends of the seven-bedroom house.

He stepped inside as his phone chimed with a text from Delaney.

Gathering case files. Have you checked the Templeton case already? Most recent threat on news.

Rebecca watched him expectantly from the kitchen counter. "Is it about the case?"

"Yes." He passed both the kitchen and the desk and rested his duffel on the coffee table in front of the leather couch. "We have a place to start at least."

The tablet's case allowed him to set the screen upright. It didn't take long to pull up the newscasts about Templeton. The man had been convicted of drug trafficking across state lines. He'd attracted national attention when he'd threatened the judge on court camera, claiming he was going to find Judge Linn's family when he got out. As far as Kurt knew, the man was still in jail. But like every other case they would look at, there would be a possibility that the prisoner could've ordered the job.

Rebecca sat on the couch cushion beside him and held her tea mug in both hands. The smell of chamomile and honey took the edge off the tension in his shoulders.

He tapped on the link Delaney had messaged him. The video captured Templeton interrupting the judge, yelling over the judge's questions and finally, issuing the threat.

Rebecca shivered. "Grandpa stayed so calm despite that man goading him, threatening him...us."

He hated this part of the job. She'd just been put under a lot of strain and here he was asking her to listen to more threats against her family. "Your grandfather wouldn't want you worrying about him. The judge is known for having nerves of steel."

She blew on the top of her mug. "I've never seen that side of him."

"To you, he's always been your grandpa."

"His name is Templeton?" She leaned back into the cushions. "His voice and eyes don't match the man who attacked me."

"No, I didn't expect him to. He's still in jail, but maybe it triggered a memory. Did your attacker mention any names? Give any hints about why they came after you?"

She shook her head. "No. Nothing."

Kurt's phone vibrated again.

Judge wants you to look at McCollum case.

He wasn't familiar with that threat. He typed in the name and the judge's name, and frowned. The incident in question happened forty years ago. In some ways, that made it more likely since the perpetrator may have been released from prison by now.

While Kurt couldn't locate any video, he found an archived news article that showed McCollum's photograph.

Rebecca leaned distractingly close, enough that he could smell the tea on her breath. Kurt cleared his throat and placed the screen back on the coffee table for her to see while keeping his distance.

Her face paled. "I recognize that man."

She set her cup down and turned away from the photo. Her finger shook as it pointed at the tablet. "I've had to look at that picture at least once a year for my entire life. My dad wanted me to always be on the lookout for him. That man is the reason my dad had to use mirrors to check underneath his car for bombs every day in high school and his entire time at college."

Kurt couldn't imagine having to live that way as a teenager.

Rebecca continued, "He's the reason why Dad moved us so far away from here, why he hardly ever came to visit Grandpa with us and why he made me promise I would never be in or get involved with anyone in law enforcement. That man doesn't need to come after us again. He's already ruined our lives."

"His rap sheet indicates he's a dangerous man. I'll get an alert out on him right away." He picked up his phone and tried to ignore the jolt he felt when she'd said she could never get involved with anyone in law enforcement. It wasn't his business, and it didn't matter. So why wouldn't his stomach unclench?

THREE

Rebecca wanted to throw the cordless phone out the window. "My name is Rebecca Linn." A nurse had called the house every few hours and asked her to recite her name as a precaution after her head injury.

"That was the last one," the nurse said. "Doctor says we can let you sleep without interruption tomorrow, but call us if you have any symptoms."

She agreed and hung up. It was hard enough to go back to sleep when it was dark, but the sun streamed through the closed curtains. Rebecca missed the gorgeous view. She'd go stir-crazy real fast if she didn't get to peek outdoors. She fought the temptation, slipped on her robe and walked into the kitchen to make some coffee.

Kurt's long form was stretched out on the leather couch with Babette purring on his stomach. Rebecca put a hand on her mouth to keep from laughing, and yet it wasn't fair. That cat refused to ever snuggle with her.

He'd changed into a short-sleeved dark polo with the golden star on the right side of his chest, dark pants and matching black socks. A pair of shoes sat on the carpet, prepped to be slipped on at a moment's notice.

He flinched and launched vertically into standing with a hand on his weapon. A small scream escaped her lips as she jumped backward. "I didn't mean to startle you." Babette had landed on her feet and seemed nonplussed.

"Are you okay?" He pivoted to scan the rest of the open space.

If she'd had any doubt that he was trained in protection, her fears dissipated. She'd never seen a man move so fast. "I couldn't sleep. I needed coffee."

His shoulders relaxed and he removed his palm from the gun at his side. Instead his hand raked over his face. "Coffee is a good idea." He slipped on his shoes before crossing into the kitchen. "So what's the prognosis?"

Understanding dawned as the daylight seeped between the blinds. "The phone calls woke you up. I'm sorry. You could've stayed in one of the guest rooms. The judge wouldn't have minded."

"Only for a moment with each call, and it's better to stay stationed closest to the entry points." He shrugged. "It's my job, so don't apologize. I'd been briefed they'd be checking on you. It's why I had you take the cordless with you to your room. I figured it was the doctor calling, but I wanted to be alert in case you told me otherwise." His brow furrowed. "I have some news. We tracked down McCollum's whereabouts around three in the morning."

Kurt had put an alert out on McCollum after her initial reaction, but he'd also insisted they review other threats. She'd reviewed mug shots until just before midnight. According to the kitchen clock, it was barely seven in the morning.

She leaned forward. "You found him?" Her breath betrayed her hopefulness. While McCollum didn't have the same eyes of her attacker, he'd been responsible for turning her father into a fearful man who didn't match the photos her grandmother, before her passing, had once showed her.

"He's dead," Kurt said.

"Oh." Her shoulders drooped. She inhaled slowly. "So it couldn't have been him." Which meant there was still a threat out there. No wonder Kurt had jumped up, ready to point his gun. Maybe it'd give her father some peace knowing the man who had first threatened Grandpa and the family was long gone. "Can I ask how?"

"Drug overdose a few years ago."

"Years ago?" To think, her dad could've been free from fear a few years ago. She sighed. "Okay. Well, give me an hour, and I'll be ready to go."

He folded his arms across his chest. "Excuse me?" Babette chose that moment to walk around his ankles, rubbing her whiskers along the hemline of his pants. Kurt rolled his eyes and tried to sidestep the cat, but instead Babette flopped on top of his shoes. "What's the cat's name again?"

"Babette."

"He's one of the bad guys in *Lady and the Tramp*, right?"

Her mouth dropped. "No. *She's* not. And she clearly likes you." She sighed. "I need to go back to Vista Resorts and check in with their accounting department to make sense out of what I saw on the flash drive."

He stared at her long enough to make her fidget. Fugitives probably surrendered without a fight if he leveled that gaze at them. "You're very intimidating when you do that," she finally said.

"I am?" His voice betrayed his genuine surprise. He blinked several times. "Sorry. I guess I stare when I'm trying to think of the best way to say something."

"I respect a man who tries to control his tongue, but in this case, it's probably worse than if you just spit it out. My imagination is too good."

He smiled for half a second before schooling his features. "You should stay here."

Well, that wasn't what she wanted to hear. She swiveled, placed an individual coffee pod into the brewer and slipped her favorite coffee mug into the designated area. Grandpa had made it clear when he'd suggested bringing in the marshals that she could still work while being protected. She wasn't in their WITSEC program, but maybe Grandpa hadn't communicated that part when he'd requested the marshals. "As far as I know, I'm not under house arrest."

His sigh reached her ears. "Technically you're correct."

"And I'm not in the witness protection program." She picked up the mug and inhaled the savory aroma but realized it was rude to serve herself before her guest. She handed the cup to the marshal. "I assume you drink it black." His face fell so fast she almost laughed. He was cute when he let his feelings show.

She pointed over his shoulder. "There's creamer in the fridge and sugar in the pantry."

"Thank you." He picked the cat off his shoe and set her to the side. Babette objected with a sniff and left the room. He crossed the room to the fridge. "It's easier to protect you while you're inside."

"Which I've given a lot of thought, really. So far, that man only tried to abduct me. Not kill me. And I'm confident no one will try that again with you by my side." She brewed her own cup of coffee and hesitated to speak aloud the thoughts that kept her awake. "He could've got me."

"What?"

Rebecca didn't want to turn and look at him for fear the tears would return. "I know you brushed it off before, but I'm sure of it. Like I tried to explain, I can't help but think he let me get away. He could've chased me down in that driveway or even got to me in that ditch. A skinny, unarmed, teenage boy waiting with me would be no match. The way the man fought, even, was almost as if he'd done it many times before. I either injured him more than I thought with the letter opener, or he let me get away." She chanced a glance.

The edge of Kurt's fingers turned white from the intensity of his grip around the mug. "And you think it has something to do with the flash drive?"

"I have no idea. It's something that doesn't make sense. Either way, I have to do my job and figure out what it means. The audit won't be submitted until I have the surety that I've looked under every rock. My mind won't rest until I've double-checked. I suspect one of the accountants slipped me the first drive. If it is connected, then the accountant might lead us to the threat."

Kurt set his mug down and put his fists on his hip. "If you're right and the threat is with the resort, that would be more the police's jurisdiction."

"But you won't know until we find out, right?"

He looked up at the ceiling. "Fine. But I'm driving."

She moved a little slower than she'd have liked. The bruises had darkened and her neck still smarted whenever she turned her head too fast, but she still managed to get ready to leave a couple hours later. Kurt had changed back into a dress shirt and slacks. Without the logo proudly displayed, she never would've guessed he was a marshal.

He helped her get in the truck and she waved goodbye to the officers when they left. Even once they'd arrived at the corporate offices, Kurt asked her to wait until he came around the other side to open the door. It was an act of protection, but either way she appreciated the gesture. He'd parked facing the view of the bright blue lake surrounded by majestic mountains topped with snow. She'd missed that sight, even if it'd been only a day cooped up inside the house.

They crossed the lot, side by side, as the breeze blew her hair back. Normally she welcomed the sensation, as her curls had the uncanny knack for sticking to her neck. Her scalp objected and she winced.

Kurt pivoted into action. One hand went for her back while the other gently held her forearm. "Are you okay?"

"Small discomfort." She used her other hand to cradle the back of her head. She'd wanted to go without the bandage as it had stopped bleeding, but maybe that had been a bad idea. They walked through the curving sidewalks, underneath the array of trees and past a stone bench.

While the landscaping had a classic design, the corporate offices portrayed innovation and design. The hotel and spa towered in the distance. Vista's main holdings were all in Coeur d'Alene with a smaller ski resort in Colorado.

A young man in a gray security uniform opened the door. His metal name tag said S. Howard. "Miss Linn. Good to see you again."

They'd struck up a nice conversation during lunch yesterday about staying in touch with relatives who lived far away. He'd given her a great idea about where to find cheap souvenirs. Meeting new people was her favorite part of the job. Grandpa, ever the introvert, didn't understand that.

The guard smiled at Kurt, but his face fell just as fast as Kurt leveled a distrustful glare at him. Rebecca almost rolled her eyes, but she supposed making people want to keep their distance was part of the protection detail, as well.

A waist-high potted plant was on either side of the door. They were placed strategically every ten feet or so around the hallways of the entire building. They made her feel like she was headed to the spa because they all looked like mini palm trees, called dracaena. Sadly all the ones inside were fake, silk leaves with white rocks surrounding them instead of dirt.

She strode across the white marble floor to the elevator, but a middle-aged woman practically chased her down. The slaps of her heeled shoes echoed in the cavernous lobby. "Miss? Miss!" The lady smoothed out her skirt when Rebecca stopped. "I'm afraid you need to stay in the waiting area."

It didn't escape her notice that Kurt's hand twitched, ready to grab the gun holstered underneath his blazer.

"Excuse me?" Maybe the lady didn't recognize her. "I was here yesterday. I'm the auditor."

"Rebecca," a male voice called out. A bald but youthful-looking man in a suit held his hand over his head and waved. If memory served her, he was the managing director and, more importantly, one of Grandpa's favorite golfing buddies. He crossed the lobby with an outstretched hand. As he shook her hand, he leaned forward to deliver a conspiratorial whisper. "We were under the impression you'd finished the on-site work." He did a double-take when he noticed Kurt but recovered. "Jake Putnam."

Kurt accepted his handshake but didn't offer his name or reason for being there. "Jake, I thought I was done, but I need to confirm something in the accounting department."

He folded his hands and pulled his mouth to the side. "See, that's where we run into a little problem. We scheduled a training day for the accountants." He tapped his index fingers to his mouth and shook his head. "We had plans to update the software. So I'm sure you understand."

Rebecca knew stall tactics when she heard them. She smiled back but didn't move from her position at the elevator. She mimicked Jake's folded hands because, according to a study her boss frequently cited, acting like a behavioral chameleon in negotiations was supposed to increase her odds of success. "That's interesting. While I did say I had what I needed yesterday, I was told to holler if I needed anything else. In fact, I was scheduled to be in the department all week long. No one knew I'd finish early. So…"

The director's face scrunched up in concern. "I wish I could help you."

So much for the supposed study.

Mr. Putnam's forehead looked particularly shiny. "The plans probably got moved up suddenly when you announced you were finished. How about I find out if Mr. Cabell can move some of these trainings around and call you?"

While it was possible they'd moved the training up suddenly, she found it hard to believe. "That'd be great."

Kurt led her to the front door. "That guy is nervous about something, I'll give you that."

Outside, a woman in a light cardigan sweater and navy pants sat on the bench and pulled a sandwich from a brown bag. Rebecca could picture exactly which cubicle she worked at in the accounting department. She worked right across from the man who'd bumped into her in the hallway.

"Excuse me?" Rebecca rushed toward her. "Remember me? Rebecca Linn." The woman nodded, so she pressed on. "I heard you guys were in training all day."

The woman raised her eyebrows. "Nothing on the schedule as far as I know."

So Mr. Putnam had been lying. Rebecca looked over her shoulder and gave Kurt a knowing nod. "Okay, well I had a quick question. Could you tell me the name of the other accountant—about my height, super-dark curly hair, wore a polo yester—"

"Levi Garner. Yeah. He apparently went on a vacation all of a sudden."

Kurt stepped forward. "Is that odd?"

The woman set her sandwich on her lap. "I don't know. Maybe just to me. He said he wanted to save up his time off so he could go on a three-week trip to Australia."

Dread settled in Rebecca's gut. The memory of the cold eyes of her attempted kidnapper gave her chills. She had the worst feeling the accountant wasn't on vacation. If her attacker was connected to the audit, Levi could be on the run or perhaps he never got to go at all.

Kurt pulled out of the parking lot, his GPS already guiding him. Rebecca spoke a mile a minute, her arms flailing beside him. He blew out a breath. "Would you please calm down? We don't know that this Levi guy has been kidnapped. For now, let's assume he's safely enjoying some sunshine down under."

"Maybe he had to go on vacation because he knew they would come after him as a whistle-blower."

"Whistle-blower to what?"

She pursed her lips. "I'm not a hundred percent sure. If I'd had just one more minute with that spreadsheet before…" Her voice trailed off.

He didn't blame her for not wanting to talk about the abduction attempt again. And there was no point in jumping to conclusions. It still seemed most likely that the threat was court related. While some of what she'd experienced was odd, so was life. Weird coincidences happened all the time. "You can stop worrying. I've already agreed that we can go talk to him." The man's address had been easy to locate and, if she could get what she needed for her auditing job, she'd be able to focus more on the threat or decide to go back to Ohio.

A shape in the rearview mirror caught his attention. A beefed-up black Hummer drove two cars behind them. It wasn't anything to worry about, but vehicles like that always made him stop and shake his head. Such overkill.

The Hummer passed one of the cars. Kurt frowned. That had been an awfully tight spot the Hummer had squeezed into. So far no laws had been broken, and while he had never given someone a traffic ticket before, he knew he had the legal backing to do so if necessary.

As he drove through another intersection, the car behind him turned right. Great. Mr. Running Late would likely tailgate him. He wouldn't allow anyone to follow too closely while with his protectee. The GPS informed him he would be making a left turn onto the US-95 bridge. Unfortunately the Hummer stayed right behind him.

Kurt sped up to create distance. He squinted in the rearview mirror and memorized the plate number. If this guy tried anything, he'd report it to the police.

"I hate bridges," Rebecca said.

Kurt chanced a glance to see her head leaning against the headrest. She was staring at the roof of the cab. He supposed the thirty, maybe forty, foot drop down to the Spokane River could make some people nervous.

The Hummer flashed a left turn signal. "You've got to be kidding me," Kurt muttered. On the one hand, the use of the signal relaxed him. Criminals didn't usually have the decency to signal what they were about to do. But on the other hand, this wasn't a passing lane. Thankfully there was no one else on the bridge.

He slid as far over to the right of the lane as he could without scraping against the two thin white guardrails. Every law-enforcement number in the area had been programmed into his phone. "Call nonemergency police." He wasn't going to take time to stop the guy in his personal vehicle while he had his protectee, but he wanted to alert the police. His phone, connected to a hands-free system, started ringing.

The truck lurched into the guardrail. "What—" He fought with the steering wheel as the sound of crunching metal filled the cab of the pickup. Rebecca gasped, but as he turned to look, the airbag opened to within an inch of his face, hitting his forearms and forcing his hands off the wheel as it fully inflated. The Hummer gave a final shove and the pickup flipped over the rail.

Rebecca's screams barely registered as the pounding of his heart filled his ears. They dangled like rag dolls against the seat belts as they vaulted through the expanse toward the unforgiving water below. The waves grew closer and closer.

"Lord, please!"

He echoed Rebecca's plea but didn't have time to say anything else except to shout, "Protect your head!"

He thrust his arms up in front of his face as the front end slapped into the water. The pickup flipped to the side and Kurt's head and torso flung into the driver's-side door. Pain blinded him as his shoulder wrenched from its socket.

The truck rolled again and his entire body hung against the seat belt. The sound of rushing water filled the back seat.

"Kurt! Kurt, are you okay? Should I open the door? Roll down the window?" Her questions came out like fast cries that he could barely comprehend while in agony. The statistics of water crashes had been drilled into his head. They had thirty, maybe ninety, seconds at the most before they lost any chance of survival.

The ache traveled across his entire left side until he couldn't take it any more. He sucked in a deep breath, twisted his arm and pulled it over his head. An unstoppable moan wrenched past his lips as the shoulder popped back into place. He blinked despite the lingering pain. At least his left side didn't feel like it was on fire anymore. He could work past sore and tender.

They hung upside down with all the windows and doors engulfed in water. Cracks covered the windshield, but as the glass was coated with a type of laminate to keep it from shattering, that wouldn't help them. The doors wouldn't budge until they stopped sinking and reached equilibrium.

He didn't know the depth of the river, but since Lake Coeur d'Alene drained into it, there was a chance it was up to two hundred feet deep. Even once the truck filled fully with water, it would take longer than they could hold their breaths before they'd be able to escape. And if they somehow did, the frigid waters would render them unconscious within fifteen minutes.

One problem at a time.

The pressure around the side windows would keep them from rolling down. He unbuckled his seat belt and caught himself on the dash. His shoulder immediately objected. Water poured in from underneath the steering wheel. The liquid, even colder than he'd imagined, seeped through his shoes and socks and set his teeth on edge.

"Kurt, what do we do?" Her eyes were wide with panic. "I can't get my seat belt off." A streak of blood dripped down her neck.

Please let it only be from aggravating the previous wound, Lord. A static-filled hum and a voice on low volume came through the speakers. Over and over, someone asked, "Sir? Sir?" The police must have connected with his cell phone.

"If you can hear me, send help to the Spokane River Bridge." He bent over at an awkward angle and yanked the keys out of the ignition before the water reached it. He flipped open the attached multifunctional tool. He made small movements toward Rebecca, knowing the seconds ticked faster than he could keep up.

"Lean on me," he instructed.

She pressed her hands on either side of his collarbone and shoved her feet against the dashboard as she pressed herself upward into the seat, so the seat belt would have more slack and room for him to maneuver. "Hurry. I can't stay like this much longer. I'm not strong enough."

He slipped the knife between her torso and the nylon webbing. They had to already be approaching a minute. His hands worked furiously until the knife flung toward him, free of its constraint. He dropped the blade as she fell against him. They fought against the tangle of arms and legs in such a small spot. He balanced himself against the dash and ripped off his blazer in preparation for the onslaught of water.

Rebecca wrapped her arms tight around her torso and shivered, her feet submerged. "It's filling fast."

The side windows were made from a different glass than the windshield. They were tempered glass. "I'm going to have to break the window. The moment I do, you need to swim out no matter what I'm doing. It's going to be hard, but it's the only way. You have to trust me."

Her lips trembled. She nodded but said nothing.

If they got out alive, he would buy window-breaking tools in bulk and give them to everyone he knew for Christmas presents. But he didn't have one now, so that wouldn't help, and the myth that unhooked headrests had been designed to the do the job had been disproven. If he had more time and if his shoulder wasn't hurting, he would've tried anyway. Kurt gulped. Almost ninety seconds. If he waited any longer they'd have no chance.

He pulled out his handgun, the very worst and last option. "Cover your ears and remember what I said. Dive into the oncoming water." Kurt pointed the weapon at the lower corner of the side window. He needed to get Rebecca out first.

The truck shifted, sinking faster. No more time for second-guessing. No room for error. He tilted his head against his good shoulder and used his other hand to cover his left ear. "Help this work," he whispered, as a prayer, and pressed the trigger.

The deafening noise made him flinch. The window shattered at the same time the water rushed in like a tsunami. Kurt sucked in a deep breath and shoved Rebecca toward the opening as he launched himself behind her.

He kicked madly against the current and lost his grip on the back of her shirt. He could feel the current of the truck sinking like a brick, pulling them down with it. Dark, murky water swirled past him as he kicked harder, fighting to the surface. He'd lost sight of Rebecca. Had she been pulled further under? His lungs burned.

His face crested and he eagerly sucked in a breath of air. His head spun and he fought against the dizziness.

Rebecca. He needed to go back down and find her. Coughing stopped him. He spun around. Wet hair clung to her cheeks and neck as another coughing fit overcame her. She began to sink.

He lunged toward her and put an arm underneath hers for support as he treaded water, shivering. "Are you okay?"

She coughed once more and nodded rapidly.

"We made it," she cried. Her teeth chattered. She closed her eyes and shook her head. "You see why I hate bridges?"

He barked a laugh. "This happens to you often, does it?" He couldn't help it. He got sarcastic when fear got the best of him. And despite all his training, this was the closest call he'd ever had. He tried to gauge which bank would be the closest. He tensed his muscles, trying to fend off the violent shivering his insides had already started.

Rebecca turned and clung to his neck as her entire body shook. "Wh-what happened, though? A pothole? A tire blowout or a freak accident?" Sirens filled the air.

Kurt met her gaze and positioned himself to start the sidestroke toward land. They needed to start moving before the cold won. He afforded himself a glance at the bridge far above them. "That was no accident. Someone wanted you dead."

And he needed to get her to safety before they tried again.

FOUR

"I can swim!" Rebecca yelled, but her plea didn't seem to do much good.

Kurt had an arm across her stomach and had dipped underwater, kicking a powerful sidestroke. He popped his head up to suck in a breath.

"Let go," she hollered again. The effort to yell actually helped keep her teeth from chattering. She shivered as he released his hold around her torso and moved his hand to her arm.

He blinked and treaded water. "Am I hurting you? I can use a straight-arm, collar-tow rescue instead."

She closed her eyes to process his words. It didn't help. She had no idea what he was talking about, but she didn't need to be rescued anymore. He'd already done a better job than any lifeguard. "I can swim," she repeated. "It'll help me stay warm. Please." Her bones had begun the process of turning into icicles. Thinking warm thoughts didn't help much when snowcapped mountains lined the valley.

"You have a head injury."

True, but she'd also heard Kurt's bloodcurdling moan in the truck as it sank. She hadn't been thinking very straight in the heat of the moment, but she'd seen him yank his shoulder back into place. He couldn't be feeling the best, either. "Don't get me wrong, I don't want you to leave without me, but I'm not woozy. If someone is trying to kill us, I'd rather you stay above water and keep a lookout."

Besides, if he lost consciousness with the extra effort of swimming while in pain, she'd have to try to rescue him. And since she'd never moved past level three of swimming lessons, he'd probably die. "Let's swim side by side. Just don't go too fast."

"As far as keeping a lookout, I've got the license plate number, and there can't be too many Hummers in the area. We've all but got this guy, Rebecca." His eyes darted to the empty section of railing on the bridge and then the bank far in the distance. Sirens grew closer. "Help is on the way."

The soothing words didn't help her chilled bones. Logically she understood that someone had tried to kill them. But she hadn't witnessed it. She'd had her eyes closed when she'd felt the impact. A few seconds later, her body felt beat-up and she was hanging upside down in a truck surrounded by water.

Her heart beat against her chest remembering the brief fight against claustrophobia. The threat had escalated from kidnapping to a murder attempt. Maybe someone from the prisons had put out a hit on her. She couldn't handle that thought yet, so she fought to focus on her breathing, her movements and everything in the present moment. "Why does anyone do the polar bear swim for fun?"

He all but growled, "Keep moving."

She kicked her legs but wasn't willing to submerge

her face again. A police cruiser and an ambulance drove slowly down the bumpy hill next to the bridge, heading their way. She held up an arm and waved, just to be sure they'd spotted them.

Kurt shifted into a breaststroke and stayed by her side, so close that her arm kept bumping into his shoulder whenever she tried to do the front crawl. "I'm not going to drown. You can give me some space." The exasperation came through loud and clear in her voice. "Thank you, though," she amended, forcing her voice to sound gentle.

"It's my job," he replied.

She bristled. It felt more personal than a job description. "You saved my life. At the very least, you've earned my gratitude as well as my grandfather's."

"I hope he sees it that way," he said with teeth clenched.

It took her a second to connect the dots. Kurt felt guilty? "It was my idea to go look for—"

"Believe me, I won't fail to mention that."

Her jaw dropped, which was unfortunate as a little bit of bitter river water sloshed into her mouth. She sputtered and he put an arm around her waist before she could object. She patted his strong forearm, but he didn't let go.

He took over kicking as she coughed a few more times. The water rushed past her, much faster than when she'd been swimming. Once her lungs were clear, she finally replied, "Well, you're not the only one who has a job to do."

Kurt didn't respond. He only kicked harder. EMTs and police officers sprinted to the bank as they reached the sloping, muddy embankment. Hands reached for her arms and pulled her up to standing before she could even try to find her footing.

The next few minutes passed in a blur as a heavy charcoal-colored blanket encased her shoulders and she was led away to the ambulance. Someone jogged backward in front of her, trying to shine a light in her eyes. "I'm fine," she cried. "Just a little sore."

"We'll see."

They let her sit in the back of the ambulance as they examined her, cleaned and re-stitched her head injury. "I'm telling you, I'm fine."

"We can't leave until the deputy marshal gives us the all clear," one technician said.

"I don't need to be admitted."

Kurt had a similar blanket draped across his shoulders, but he was allowed to pace across the grass. His lips moved, but he spoke in low tones to the police officers so she couldn't make out what he was saying.

"Unbelievable!" He repeated the word four times in a row, each time with a little more force.

So whatever they'd been talking about couldn't have been good. A black SUV barreled down the hill at a much faster speed than the emergency vehicles crews. Kurt's eyes sought hers as he strode toward the ambulance. "That's our ride. Are you sure you don't need to go to the hospital?"

"Positive."

The SUV pulled up next to them and rolled down the window, US Deputy Marshal Delaney Patton at the wheel. She looked so professional in dress pants, a dress shirt, a blue US Marshals jacket and a cap with her hair neatly arranged out of the back opening. "Rebecca, it'd be safer if you get in while we wait. This has bulletproof and tinted windows."

Kurt opened the back door. "No need to wait. I'll be ready in just a second."

Rebecca passed on her many thanks to the two men in the back of the ambulance as she slipped inside. The vents blasted heat, which helped ease the chill but didn't take away the horrible feeling of her wet clothes sticking to her skin. Delaney rolled up her jacket sleeves. Only up close could she see the sweat beaded on her forehead.

Rebecca welcomed the thoughtfulness as her body finally relaxed.

"Sorry to meet again in these circumstances," Delaney said. "I heard you've had a rough afternoon. Good thing this ride arrived today. Too bad it didn't come sooner. That Hummer would've had a much harder time with this bulletproof—" She broke off when Kurt hopped into the vehicle. He grunted as he reached over to put on his seat belt.

Delaney barreled up the steep, rocky incline. "I can get you back to the house in under five minutes."

He nodded but said nothing.

The heat seemed to jar Rebecca's thoughts loose and questions tumbled out of her mouth faster than she could filter them. "How's my grandfather? Did someone try to hurt him? What about my parents? My brother? My niece? Have any attempts been made on any of them?"

"No," Delaney answered first. "That's the short version. We've already been in contact with law enforcement in both locations. The judge is fine and, as far as your parents are concerned, my understanding is they still have no knowledge of the threat, but they are being closely monitored and will be informed if we find a potential threat in their vicinity."

Kurt gestured to the unopened water bottles in the console. His face had lost the hard edge of anger. He lifted one bottle and turned around to offer Rebecca one. She accepted and greedily gulped it down. "Slowly," he encouraged. "I wasn't talking to you, Delaney. You should speed to your heart's content."

Delaney laughed. "No need. We're already here." She waved at the two police cruisers tucked behind bushes on either side of the driveway and pulled into the garage. They followed the same protocol as the first time Kurt had brought her to the judge's house.

They stepped inside and since Rebecca had lost her shoes underwater, her stocking-covered feet made instant wet spots on Grandpa's floors.

"I'm heading back to help coordinate the search efforts, but I'm taking my own ride," Delaney said. "I signed out weapons for you. They're in the trunk." She handed Kurt the keys. "A new duffel bag with a standard-issue uniform is in the living room. The police are willing to add a couple more officers to the perimeter, but they're pretty taxed already."

Rebecca marveled at Delaney's efficiency, but Kurt merely shook his head. "Please tell me you have good news."

"Only news I have is the same as the police so far. The plate number you gave me was twenty years old. The original owner said the tags had been on his Isuzu truck, which he dropped off at a junkyard five years ago."

Kurt placed a hand over his eyes. "How does a Hummer just disappear?"

"It's a small town—"

"Exactly."

"And," Delaney said, "there is a lot of forest across that bridge, a lot of places to hide in any of the foothills surrounding us. We'll find it. Just give it a little more time." She strode to the connecting door to the garage. "I'll have an officer courier you a new phone as soon as I get one cleared from the IT department. He's almost done scanning Miss Linn's, as well. The landline is secure, so feel free to call me on it." She waved and disappeared inside the garage.

"You know what else is over that bridge," Rebecca said. She fought against shivering.

Kurt turned his head ever so slightly and met her gaze. "Don't say it."

"Levi Garner's house."

"I can't believe you said it." He walked over to the duffel bag and bent to pull out what looked like official logo sweatpants and sweatshirt. "I let you talk me into a wild-goose chase once already against my better judgment because, as you pointed out, it had been a kidnapping attempt not a threat on your life. But this—"

"It wasn't a wild-goose chase. It was for my job. And I understand your concern, but surely if this is on the news they'll track down the Humm—"

Kurt turned to look her directly in the eye. "The media will only know there's been an accident on that bridge, Rebecca. Nothing more. Select law enforcement know what really happened today, but your name was kept out of it."

His voice, soft and low, was almost enough to lose her train of thought. The exhaustion from the last hour had to be catching up to her because she couldn't help but think he'd be excellent at reading bedtime stories. She cleared her throat. "Can I ask—"

He strode past her on his way to the guest bathroom. "Your grandfather made it clear he wanted the threat to stay out of the media for the time being, and I agree. Most people don't know what their local federal judges even look like, which serves the judges and the Marshals well. If the attention is put on you, your grandfather, or this house, then the risk only increases."

"Because of the other threats out there?"

"Exactly. Most crimes are ones of opportunity. Let's not give anyone else ideas."

She stared at a spot on the wall behind him and her mind took her back to that moment, yet again, when the attacker had grabbed her. "What color was the Hummer?"

"Black."

She should've remembered it before, remembered to mention it. "I saw a boxy, black SUV in the front yard that night…"

His eyes flashed for a second before he gestured at the blanket around her shoulders. "I recommend you get warm and dry. If you're up for it, it's more important than ever to get through the rest of the potential threat list since…" His shoulders rose ever so slightly as he shook his head and never finished his sentence.

Rebecca didn't need to ask him to finish, though, because she already knew. Someone wanted her dead now, and it didn't seem to matter who else they killed to finish the job.

* * *

Kurt wiped the fog off the mirror. Bags appeared underneath his eyes. Usually after a fugitive tracking, he was given some extra R & R, but under the circumstances, vacation time didn't seem to be coming any time soon.

The hunt for an outlaw was mentally, and sometimes physically, demanding, but his emotions usually didn't come into play—except when circumstances involved children. He'd seen a lot of hard things and been put in many dangerous situations, but he'd never been taken off guard before.

The hot water had loosened some of the knots in his back and, thankfully, seemed to help his shoulder. His stomach wouldn't unclench, though. He'd almost lost her. He was used to working alone, living alone. Usually it served him well, but Rebecca seemed to want him to act like a partner even though she wasn't a marshal and had no law-enforcement experience. He understood the desire to help, but it made more sense for her to keep her head down and to focus on identifying her attacker from the safety of the secured house. The tension in his gut tightened as if calling him out.

Maybe if he had been more open with her, he would've pointed out the bad driving of the Hummer behind him. There was a small possibility she would've recognized it and he could've maneuvered to avoid the hit. Or not.

If he started voicing every potential danger while he was guarding her, she'd turn into a walking mess of fear. Bottom line: he needed backup. But they were short staffed. Most of the other deputy marshals in the area were out on other fugitive operations. After today, he hoped the Judicial Security Inspector would divert more resources their way.

Maybe it was time to settle down and get out of the field. The current inspector in the region would be retiring soon and there was an opening for chief deputy marshal. Either was a senior position he knew he'd want someday if he ever had a family—a highly unlikely event—but the sudden desire unnerved him.

The phone rang from the living room. He groaned. "Please don't answer that," he hollered from inside the door. The hospital had stopped making calls, so it was probably Delaney giving him a status report. Hopefully they'd found the Hummer. If they found a way to identify the attacker, half the battle was done. He could track anyone.

"We might miss it," she hollered back. "Your partner took the answering machine, remember?"

If the call was from anyone other than Delaney, he didn't want her answering it. Was she expecting a phone call on her grandfather's landline? They hadn't touched on any potential personal threats, perhaps from a former relationship. He grumbled at the thought but finished dressing in a heartbeat and slid in his socks across the floor to the kitchen phone.

Rebecca's fingernails tapped on the countertop as she watched him with an amused smile. Her grin took him by surprise and he misjudged the distance and bumped into the counter. Not having a cell phone was unacceptable. He hoped the IT guys at the courthouse were able to deploy him a new one fast.

"Marshal Brock."

"It's about time," the elderly voice snapped.

Kurt stiffened. So the judge knew about the bridge

incident. Kurt needed to remember that the judge didn't sign his paychecks, though Justice Linn could make his current station unpleasant while he was in town. "Sir—"

"The rookie already updated me. And while I'm disappointed you didn't keep the situation from happening, I'm thankful you kept my granddaughter safe. Please put her on."

Kurt pulled the receiver away slightly, unsure of what had just happened. He'd anticipated a verbal thrashing, but instead had got a pat on the back. Not what he'd expected. He shoved the phone at Rebecca before he had the clarity to answer the judge. "Yes, sir," he said loudly as an afterthought.

Rebecca raised an eyebrow before placing the phone to her ear. "Grandpa, before you say anything, I'm okay."

She'd changed into blue jeans and a light pink sweater draped over a brown T-shirt. It was a dramatic transformation from the hospital gown and business suit he'd seen her in so far. Her curly hair, while still wet, framed her face and made her eyes seem even bigger.

"No, I'm not going back yet," Rebecca said. "Are *you* planning to come home?" She turned her back to Kurt as she spoke into the phone.

He strained his ears just in time to hear the judge say his Boise protection detail was very competent.

"Exactly. Precautions are being taken, and you aren't letting fear dictate your life. Your job is important and so is mine."

He'd lost count of how many times Rebecca bristled at any potential insinuation that her occupation wasn't as important as others. While he found it honorable to care about a job well done, he wondered where the passion came from about auditing, of all things. In fact, she had an unnerving capability to be energetic about everything.

The judge's voice grew loud enough that Kurt overheard snippets of the elderly man's side of the conversation.

"You always taught me a fair judge never makes assumptions." She twisted around and pressed her fingertip into the countertop as she made her point. "My job is important to me, to my company and to the backers looking to invest their hard-earned money. I'm making sure justice happens in my own way."

The judge chuckled and said something about a chip off the old block and that he wouldn't dare argue against that. Kurt marveled at Rebecca's ability to put the hard-edged man at ease, especially given the situation.

"What about the marshal?" The crackly voice came through the receiver.

"I'm in excellent hands."

Kurt's chest expanded. He didn't need compliments, but they always felt great to hear.

The judge's voice was garbled and Kurt almost didn't hear the response, but it had something to do with her spending time with him. A light blush washed over Rebecca's cheeks as her lips fought back a smile.

She averted her eyes from Kurt. "Tolerable, I suppose."

He crossed his arms. What was that supposed to mean? A mere second ago she'd put her grandfather in his place for judging things he didn't have the whole story on and then she had the audacity to rate time with him as tolerable when he'd risked his life—

"You're comparing him to Mr. Darcy?" the judge practically shouted over the line. His words were clear as day even seven feet away from the phone.

Kurt's forehead relaxed. That name—Mr. Darcy—sounded familiar.

"I knew you fell asleep during the movie! You definitely weren't resting your eyes," Rebecca shot back. "Darcy actually said that about Elizabeth. If you don't remember what he said next, you're going to have to look it up."

Kurt didn't know about the judge, but as soon as he had a smartphone back that was exactly what he intended to do.

"It should put your mind at ease," Rebecca continued. "Everyone involved is top-notch and doing a wonderful job. So I'll let you get back to work, Grandpa, and I'll get back to mine." She paused for a second. "Love you, too." She held out the receiver to Kurt. "Back to you."

Standing by a landline phone felt like going back into time. "Sir?"

"My granddaughter feels there is a chance this is work related. Between you and me, if it is, she can go back to Ohio without bringing the threat with her, so follow any leads you have and get this done. You need to be one hundred percent sure, though. Understood? I have to be back in court. Goodbye."

The judge hung up before Kurt could respond. His blood heated to close to a boil. He wasn't the type of guy who had to be in charge, but he also wasn't one to take orders, especially vague ones. The job description of a deputy marshal wasn't the same as a baby-sitter or chauffeur. He would never presume to know the judge's job. It irked him that people without experience in law enforcement thought they knew better.

Rebecca beamed. "Well, we've agreed. I should get back to work, which means it's time to hunt down Levi Garner."

Why'd he let this woman get under his skin? He took a deep breath. "You may talk your way out of anything with your grandfather, but I'm not related to you. First, we analyze the risks."

"But—"

He crossed his arms over his chest. "You do understand we could've died back there, right?"

Her nose crinkled when she frowned. "I had complete faith in you."

While the words soothed his pride after her little comment about being tolerable, he wanted to stress his point. "Well, let's not test that faith. Let's get back to work. Based on Judge Linn's cases, we have some hate groups that operate in Northern Idaho that we need to rule out."

Although, if he could confirm the vehicle she'd seen on the night of the kidnapping attempt was the Hummer, maybe that would rule out a coordinated effort of people after Rebecca. One person was easier to catch.

The doorbell rang. "Stay back, please." He walked to the door. As much as he hated to admit it, the prudent thing to do would be to rule out a potential threat from Rebecca's work.

An officer at the door handed him a bag from the IT department at work.

Rebecca peeked around the corner as Kurt closed

the door with two phones in hand. "They couriered over a phone for me," he explained. "It seems your phone is cleared. He wants a little more time with your laptop."

"No spyware on the phone?"

"Usually our IT guy, Mike, would've alerted one of us if it was a concern. So, you're free to use it, but I have some requests." He handed the cell to her. "Until the threat is gone, use it for emergencies only. Put my number in your contacts and give me permission to find your location if for some reason we get separated when we leave. Turn off all other location services and permissions. Ignore any other texts or emails for now. If you feel you must return one, I need to know how you're wording it to make sure you don't give away any pertinent information that might hinder our efforts."

"Fine. You said, 'When we leave.' Where?"

"For Levi Garner's house."

His heart skipped a beat as her eyes widened—he could get lost in those eyes. She smiled, and he had the irrational desire to kiss her. One way or another, this assignment was going to be the death of him.

FIVE

"True confession time. I wanted to be a detective when I grew up." Rebecca sent a shy smile to Kurt in the front of the truck.

He flashed her a lopsided grin. "Why does that not surprise me?" His eyes darted from the rearview mirror to the side mirror, and he kept his hands tight around the steering wheel.

Despite her objections, they'd been forced to wait until morning to visit Levi Garner. The bridge had to be repaired, since there was no other way across the river unless they wanted to drive over an hour around the lake, and Kurt had refused to take her out after dark. She just hoped the accountant was there. She called the resort's corporate offices and Levi's number again before they'd left in the event he'd returned. He hadn't.

Her audit couldn't be submitted in good faith without following through on the flash drive. More than that, she needed proof she hadn't imagined the numbers.

Rebecca had yet to admit it to anyone, but the fear that she'd invented the highlighted rows and the scratch on the flash drive had plagued her nightmares for the second night in a row. It terrified her that falling on those rocks might've done more damage than a headache and sore muscles. She needed to be able to trust her thoughts and memory or she wouldn't be fit to work, not as an auditor, at least.

Still, the extra rest seemed to have done the handsome deputy some good. His eyes looked clearer, without the reddened signs of water or lack of sleep. "You didn't pursue becoming a detective because of your father?" he asked.

She shrugged. "If you think about it from a different perspective, being an auditor is kind of like being a detective. Numbers, like hard evidence, don't lie. Either everything adds up or I go after the truth until it does."

"So you like it."

"Yeah. I guess." Did she? She hadn't taken time lately to evaluate it. "I wanted to see more of the country. So when I found out there was such a thing as a traveling accountant, it sounded like a great option. I've been to almost every major city in the country and lots of small towns."

"Favorites?"

"Uh… I don't know. I try hard to see the sights before I leave, but to be honest, the majority of the time I'm inside a hotel or airplane."

"I travel a lot, too. I get it."

She believed him. For a man of such few words, it surprised her that he'd admitted that much. "Did you always want to be a marshal?"

"No." His jaw tensed.

The man went back and forth from being warm

and vulnerable to short and closed-off faster than a speeding bullet.

Rebecca couldn't decide if it was his natural personality or Grandpa's doing. When Grandpa had asked her last night if Kurt was being friendly, she'd known exactly what the judge had meant. He wouldn't approve of any romantic inclinations between the two of them, and it would be just like Grandpa to tell Kurt to stay away.

She adored her grandfather, but he could be overly protective—one of the things her father had in common with him. It wasn't as if she was a teenager on summer break. She was a grown woman who'd been on her own for years. So it had to be the fact Kurt was in law enforcement that had prompted him to ask such a question. Unless Grandpa knew something she didn't.

At any rate, she couldn't say aloud exactly what she was thinking when Kurt had been standing three feet away. Her reference to *Pride and Prejudice* was meant to calm her grandfather down without raising Kurt's suspicions about what they were discussing.

In the movie, and probably the book if she'd ever taken the time to read it, Mr. Darcy had said that Elizabeth was "tolerable, I suppose, but not handsome enough to tempt me." And while Kurt was as good-looking as a man could be, Rebecca wanted to convey to her grandfather that it wouldn't be a problem to keep her attraction in check. Of course, the more time she spent with Kurt, the harder it was to say that truthfully.

Kurt glanced at her. "I didn't mean to be short with you or imply you should stop talking. I guess I'm not used to people asking me questions."

"It's usually the other way around?"

He nodded. "Yes. Interviewing suspects and witnesses. You might want to look at the ceiling again. We're going over the bridge, and you do not want to see their flimsy temporary fix of a guardrail."

A lump formed in her throat. "Descriptions don't help, either." She leaned her head back and closed her eyes, but she couldn't help but shift her shoulder toward the console, as far from the window as possible. "Keep my mind busy. The classical music isn't doing it."

He cleared his throat. "Okay. I served my time in the army. Didn't really know what I wanted to do when I got out, so went to college while working as a security guard. Criminal justice seemed like a good major, and I got recruited. I've been told by some of my colleagues that I had it easy. A lot of people, like Delaney, have being a marshal as their goal from the beginning of their career."

The sound from the tires on the concrete changed their pitch. "We're on solid ground," he said.

Rebecca opened her eyes. It seemed there was a lot of things unsaid from the marshal's story. She wanted to ask him all about his time in the military and in college, but those seemed like topics that only closer friends could ask. She settled on a less personal question. "Did you know you wanted to be in criminal justice before you enlisted?"

He grunted. He took a left turn on Presley Road. The trees on either side of the road petered out into farmland.

She'd pushed him too far. "We don't have to talk anymore," she said. The sunshine streamed through the windows. Being cooped up inside most of the day drove her crazy.

His shoulders relaxed. "No, it's fine. I used to play baseball. My only plan during senior year was to get a scholarship."

They passed farmhouses and the paved road turned into a dirt road. Up ahead was a hill filled with evergreens. "Are you sure you're going the right way?"

"According to the map." He pointed to a for-sale sign on the right as the incline steepened. "Anyway, the day before the first scout was due to arrive, I slid into home base wrong. Broke my ankle. Was out the rest of the season." He nodded forward. "And that's enough of the Kurt Brock Story Hour. I hope you've got sorted what questions you need to ask Mr. Garner because we're here. I want us in and out of his place in five minutes. Stay put a moment. I need to canvass the area first."

He pulled up in front of a gray house. It had a one-car garage, two windows and a metallic front door. The place couldn't be more than one or two bedrooms at the most. Kurt stepped out of the vehicle with a hand on his holster. Assuming the accountant was scared enough to stay home from work, seeing Kurt might send him running for the trees.

If Mr. Garner owned the land, he knew how to invest his money. An accountant for a resort company might pick up real estate advice naturally. From the higher vantage point on the hill, she could see the lake, evergreens in every direction and wildflowers along various dirt paths. It was almost enough to entice her to settle down.

Kurt knocked on the car as he rounded the front.

"We're clear." He opened the door for her and she stepped out. "I don't know if Garner is here or not, but it's time to find out."

"If he's not, I don't know what my next step is."

"You might need to let your boss know he should cut the Vista Resorts account loose. I've already been speaking to the marshals in Ohio in case we don't find any more leads here."

Her neck tensed. Something about that bothered her, and she couldn't place a finger on exactly what. Maybe it was the mystery of never knowing who tried to kill her, and if they would move their sights to Grandpa once she was gone. Or, maybe it was the uncertainty of the accuracy of her audit report. It couldn't be leaving Kurt. That was a ludicrous thought. She'd known the man for only a few days and, granted he'd saved her life, that didn't mean she'd automatically swoon.

She inhaled the scent of pine and her shoe crunched on an errant cone as she made her way to the door. Kurt stepped in front of her, the cedar aftershave tickling her nose. They stopped at the metallic door. He stepped closest and turned his hip away from the door so he stood at a diagonal, his hand on the holster.

Rebecca raised her fist and rapped on the door. The latch gave way underneath her knock and the door swung open. Kurt pivoted so his torso moved in between her and the house as he pulled out his gun in one smooth motion. She stepped backward, prepared to run. His shoulders sank.

"Get in the truck."

Just past his shoulders gave her an opening to see inside. Levi Garner's head was slumped forward, his hands were bound to an office chair and blood soaked his shirt. "Is he…?" Her voice shook.

Kurt kept his gun drawn and stepped sideways in a protective stance. "Rebecca," he whispered, "I need to get you in the truck. Someone might still be inside or watching." His chin pointed at the SUV. "Use the closest door."

Her pulse quickened as she finally understood. He stayed by her side until she jumped into the back seat. The moment the door closed, the locks latched. She watched him out of the darkened window as he lifted a phone to his ear. Probably calling for backup. She swiveled in her seat to hunt for any sign of the shooter. She squinted in an effort to see farther in the distance. They were only ten minutes from the heart of downtown but it still felt as if they were in the middle of nowhere. Even though the SUV was bulletproof, it didn't calm her heart.

Kurt shoved his phone back in his pocket and entered the house, his gun raised. Leaving the door open, he reached over and touched Levi's wrist. He let go and held the gun with both hands as he disappeared into the hallway of the house. No attempt to revive him or call for the paramedics. That could mean only one thing.

Levi had been murdered.

Kurt exhaled as he peeked around the corner. Clear. He kicked aside a chair next to the round table as he traveled past the combined kitchen and dining room. He repeated the process in the bathroom, the two bedrooms and the hall closet.

So far there'd been no sign of the shooter. Nothing

remarkable to catch his attention. All the walls were beige and unadorned. A clean and cozy home that for some reason made him think Levi had been a lonely guy. He retraced his steps and it hit him. The place reminded him of his own rental. He hadn't hung a single frame or painting.

Kurt refocused and made his way to the living room, a mere ten feet long and ten feet wide, and crammed with a futon, a bookshelf, a desk and TV. He barely had enough room to maneuver around the two suitcases that leaned up against the futon and almost bumped the dead man in the chair.

He stepped outdoors and heard the crunching of rocks in the distance. He'd asked the police vehicles to approach without sirens, but he couldn't make any assumption. He positioned himself equidistant from the house and SUV.

Red and blue lights crested the hill and he exhaled. He crossed to where Rebecca waited and knocked on the back door. She emerged, her arms tightly wrapped around her torso. "Why?" she whispered. "Why did the shooter tie Levi's wrists to the armrests if he was just going to shoot him anyway?"

Interrogation. It was the only reason that made sense to him. The shooter wanted to scare the accountant enough to get him talking. There was a possibility torture was involved, but without investigating the body, he couldn't be certain. These were things he had no intention of sharing with Rebecca. "Maybe they wanted to know something without the fear Levi would attack," he said instead.

"But if he gave them what he wanted, why shoot him?"

"We don't know if he did."

She put her hands on either side of her face and trembled.

Kurt put an arm around her and pulled her close before he truly knew what he was doing. "It's…it's going to be okay." She pressed into him, her head fitting perfectly underneath his chin.

Two cruisers pulled up next to him, one from the local police department and another from the County Sheriff's Office. When a murder happened in a small town, it was common to combine efforts. An officer approached. He pointed at Rebecca. "Do we need a bus?"

"They're asking if you need an ambulance," Kurt said.

Rebecca straightened, pulled her shoulders back and pushed the curls away from her eyes. "No. I'm fine."

"The victim is inside," Kurt told the officer. "We need a perimeter set up around the property in case the shooter is still on-site."

"Yes, sir." The cop strode over to speak with the others.

"I need to know if Levi was the man that gave me the flash drive." Her voice shook but her eyes had turned steely and determined. "I need a second look to be sure."

Kurt blew out a steady breath, his frustration building. "Follow me, but don't touch anything." He led her to the entryway but didn't go any farther. They'd ask about the flash drive and leave. One officer was taking photographs, another dusting for fingerprints and another taking electronic notes.

The lead investigator pointed at Kurt. "I assume you want to consult on this?"

It was actually the last thing he wanted to do. The more he got involved, the greater chance reporters would get wind of a federal judge's granddaughter being a target, but he needed to have all the facts at his disposal. "I'd like to be kept in the loop at the very least, but as I explained on the phone, she needs to stay out of the media."

"Understood. I'll have some questions for her, though."

Rebecca averted her eyes from the deceased man's form and stared at the ground. "I think this might have to do with his job at Vista Resort Properties. I think this man tried to act as a whistle-blower. I'm sure he snuck me a flash drive before he died. Is there any way I could look at his files?"

"You? No." The detective would need to rule her out as a potential suspect, even if Rebecca would be the best consultant he could find for the case. Kurt understood that and didn't argue.

"Deputy Brock will eventually get a look," the detective added. "But not until we do first. Don't get your hopes up, though. So far we don't have anything to work with. There's no phone, no computer and no flash drives. No papers, either."

"Okay, you heard him. There's no flash drive here. We can go." Kurt turned to guide Rebecca away, but she shook her head.

"This has to be about the audit," she whispered. "Think about it. They tried to kidnap me...maybe to find out what I know. Only I made it easy on them because the flash drive was plugged into the computer.

They take it and, after seeing what's on it, know they have to kill me. That's why the threat escalated."

"You're making a lot of assumptions without facts."

"Because it makes sense. So, they tried to kill us by shoving us off the bridge. Then they find the whistle-blower that gave me the information in the first place. Levi must have known something fishy was going on at the company because he had this place for sale and, judging by the luggage, he was scared and getting ready to get out of town. The guy who tried to get me interrogated him to make sure he hasn't told anyone else and then killed him and took all the evidence with him."

"That's some good out-of-the-box thinking, but we have no facts to support it." He wouldn't acknowledge that he had the same train of thought until he had some hard evidence. There was no room to assume it was the threat on Rebecca. It was possible the two incidents were completely unrelated.

"Look at the bookshelf." Rebecca leaned over the threshold and held up a finger.

The investigator studied the shelves filled with cases of video games. "He's a gamer."

"Not just any games." She waved her finger, pointing at the logo on each spine. "Look at the platform. Correct me if I'm wrong, but that has a cloud application on it."

Kurt frowned. "How do you know that?"

She shrugged. "I'm a cool aunt, hip with the times. The point is that if Levi had any spreadsheets on his personal cloud—"

"He could still be signed in and we would see those files on the console," the investigator finished for her.

"Anything he saved to the cloud might shed the light on his killer."

"Exactly." She exhaled. "It would also point the way in figuring out the truth to this audit."

The detective gestured over her shoulder, making it obvious the time had come to get out of the way of the crime scene team. Kurt's stomach felt like lead; a sure sign that something was bothering him. He wasn't sure why but knew it had to do with her hypothesis.

Yes, he liked her. And, moments ago, pulling her into his arms felt right, but he hadn't forgotten that she'd be on a plane to Ohio as soon as it was deemed safe. If the threat turned out to be from the resort, he would need to hand over most of the control to the police. He could protect her a little longer if it was the judge's desire, but their time together would be at an end. Why did that bother him so much?

An officer stepped outside holding a small card with her gloved hand. "You're Rebecca Linn? The deceased had your business card."

It was like a light switch in his head. If the killer thought he'd eliminated Rebecca, he'd know by now that he hadn't succeeded. He hadn't waited around to make sure they'd drowned or the police would've located the Hummer. Nothing had been in the news. So, if the killer had a connection to the resorts, the lack of notification to the Vista Resorts' employees that the auditor had died would also be a clue. "We need to get you back to the judge's house."

Rebecca held a hand out toward the scene. "The detective said he would have questions for me later. And we can take a closer look once they're done."

There she went again with her use of the word *we.*

If anyone was getting a closer look at the crime scene, it would be him. Not *them*. "Negative. They have my information and can contact me if they find something on the gaming console. My primary concern is your safety, and your auditing job is not dependent on staying at a murder scene. Let's go." He would call Delaney on the way back and have her track down a staff directory for Rebecca to peruse. Ideally they would have one with photographs, but if not, maybe a name would still be enough of a trigger.

She huffed and followed him back to the SUV. "But there might be something here to point us to the murderer."

Yet again another reminder why he was more suited to fugitive tracking. He couldn't force Rebecca to do anything she didn't want to do, and she didn't seem to respect his expertise in safety. "This isn't time to live out a childhood fantasy, Rebecca."

She jolted to a stop a foot from the SUV and raised an eyebrow. "When someone confides in you, it's poor form to use it against them."

He reared back. He had no intention of using anything against her. "I've never been one to share secrets, so I'm afraid I don't know how to play your game. I know how to keep you safe, and you're making it very difficult."

Her cheeks flamed and she got into the passenger seat without further argument.

Kurt started the ignition and made a three-point turn to get around the other vehicles.

"It wasn't a game." The way she stressed the last word emphasized her displeasure. "It was conversation."

He hated disappointing her, but he was also at his wit's end. "Something I'm not supposed to be doing with you in the first place."

"Why not?" She gasped. "I knew it. Grandpa told you not to talk to me, didn't he?"

"I'm not sure why that would bother you, seeing as I'm merely tolerable. Not handsome enough to tempt you." The words slipped out of his mouth and he wished he could yank them back and stuff them in his duffel bag, where they could never escape. He'd looked up the Mr. Darcy comment last night and while he had tried to brush it off as no big deal—because he shouldn't even care—it'd been bubbling underneath the surface all day.

Her cheeks flamed. "You…you understood that reference?"

Maybe they should've stayed at the crime scene, after all. It might've been safer than the territory he was about to enter.

SIX

For a split second, Rebecca considered jumping out of the vehicle and taking her chances with the shooter to avoid further embarrassment. "It's not that you aren't handsome. I mean your face…your shoulders…" No, she didn't want to start listing specifics. She held up her hand. "All the qualities, really." That didn't sound right. "I mean…" If her face heated any more it would burst into flames.

"You can stop now."

"Thank you." She dropped her forehead into her hands. She kept her head there but turned her face to study him. Patches of red lined his neck. Was he flushing or mad? She had to fix the mess she'd made. "I was trying to make the point that despite your good looks, I wouldn't be trying to start a relationship. You have to understand I was only trying to ease Grandpa's mind. My family has this thing that I should totally avoid—"

"Anyone in law enforcement. Yes, I know." He held up a hand. "It's fine. You don't need to explain. I shouldn't have said anything at all." He sighed. "And it wasn't my intention to throw something you shared in confidence back in your face. I felt it was necessary to get you to leave faster. I should've tried another tactic." He glanced at her. "Either stay down or look up. We have to go over the bridge again."

Her heart warmed at his apology and thoughtfulness. She straightened and stared at the ceiling. "You weren't entirely unjustified. I suppose I was trying to call the shots more than let you do your job. I've been told I can be stubborn if I think I'm right."

He chuckled. "Oh, really? I hadn't noticed."

She playfully slapped his shoulder. "Hey, I can say it, but you can't." She blinked rapidly. She'd just interacted with him like a friend, but he wouldn't even be with her if he wasn't on duty.

The severity of the situation hit her afresh. Her stomach churned with nausea.

"Hey, are you okay? We're almost across."

"It feels so wrong to laugh when minutes ago…" She waved her hand toward the back window but refused to let her mind dwell on Levi's body. If she did, his bloodied shirt and broken form would start playing on a loop, and she wouldn't be able to fight the tears back any longer.

"It's a coping mechanism," Kurt said, his voice soft and kind. "It doesn't take away the other feelings, but it helps handle them. We're over the bridge now."

"Thank you." Her throat tightened and her words sounded garbled. "I like facts more than feelings."

"You and me both."

She liked looking at the facts before making a decision. People thought she could be impulsive, but she didn't see it that way. She purposefully lived in the moment and made decisions fast. Did she do that to avoid feelings?

Every choice she'd made since she'd arrived came into question. Maybe if she'd been more diligent, she would've found whatever information was on the flash drive at the resort offices by herself. She'd have sent the red flag immediately to corporate, where there would be no way it could remain a secret. Levi Garner would've never had to get involved.

Then again, if she weren't ruled by living in the moment, her impulse to check what was on the flash drive would never have been acted upon. If she'd never checked the flash drive, if it hadn't already been plugged into her laptop when the man attacked her, would they have left her alone? Would they have left Levi alone?

She sucked in a deep breath. If there were files on the video game console, she'd stay to see if she could complete the audit, but if not, maybe it was best for everyone's safety to let it go and return to Ohio.

Kurt's gaze flitted over her face before he turned back to the road, his forehead creased. "It's best not to think too much about what you saw, Rebecca."

She liked the way he said her name.

"We're almost back to your grandpa's house," he said. "True confession time."

"Oh?"

"I'm kind of rooting for this to be about your audit."

"Ah. So you can get rid of me faster." She said it in a teasing tone but her throat tightened all the same. Why'd she care so much that this man like her?

His eyebrows jumped. "No, that's not it. If this has nothing to do with law enforcement, maybe your dad will see that crime can happen anywhere. If being an officer is really your dream career, it's not too late. You're not too old." He winked. "Yet."

She returned his smile, but she needed to process. He was right. Her dad wouldn't have a leg to stand on. Her career, supposedly the safest, had brought her into danger. Yet she had no desire to change careers. Her childhood dream had lost its appeal the moment she had seen Levi. After today, working with numbers sounded a lot more appealing than dealing with violence and crime.

Kurt pulled into the driveway and rolled down the window as a police officer approached.

"Justice Linn sent flowers for Miss Linn," he said.

"You made sure they were safe?" Kurt asked.

The officer pointed at the house. "Looked right down into the vase. Nothing but a little water and stems. Left them inside on the counter."

Kurt turned to her. "Does that sound like something your grandpa would do?"

She placed a hand on her neck, overwhelmed by her grandpa's gesture. "He wouldn't have ordered them himself, but it does sound like something he would ask his secretary to do." She smiled. "It's sweet." She missed Grandpa. They'd really had only one night together with his busy schedule, and that was the night they'd called in takeout and found the movie version of *Pride and Prejudice* in Grandma's old collection. Grandpa wasn't much of a movie watcher, as evidenced by his falling asleep, but it'd been fun.

Kurt drove the rest of the way into the garage. She didn't even try to exit the car first this time. He opened her door and took her hand, something he hadn't done since the first time he'd helped her into his truck. Heat traveled up her arm, and they looked into each other's eyes. Forget wanting a job in law enforcement. If the threat and danger was related to her boring accounting job, her family wouldn't be able to object to her being in a relationship with someone in law enforcement, either.

He dropped her hand like it was a hot brick, as if he'd heard her thoughts, and pulled back his shoulders. "It occurred to me, in the interest of ruling out other possible reasons for the threat, that we haven't asked you much about your personal life."

She pulled her chin back. Her personal life? "What do you need to know?"

He shrugged. "I can let you rest and have lunch first. You've had a trying day."

She followed him up the two steps to the connecting door to the house. He went first and her hand kept the door open as she stepped inside. A gorgeous red vase filled with daisies sat in the middle of the counter. She jerked to a stop at the threshold and blinked. Nope, still daisies.

Kurt eyed her. "What's wrong? What is it?"

She stood her ground and pointed. "Grandpa would never send those." Even his secretary would know enough not to send them. "We're both allergic to them."

His eyes widened. He spun her shoulders around so forcefully she almost tipped, but he pushed her lower back forward. She avoided falling on her face by leaping over the steps into the garage.

"Go! Run!"

Her back stiffened. Why? Because someone wanted her to have an allergic reaction? She wouldn't go into anaphylactic shock or anything, at least she hadn't yet. There'd be some bad hives and itchy eyes and—

Kurt barreled toward her. She couldn't make her legs move as fast as she wanted. His strong arm wrapped around her middle and lifted her into the air. A shriek escaped at the surprising force of his actions. Kurt ran with her in the air, toward the closed aluminum garage door.

It was as if the air itself compressed and turned into a powerful wall as it hit her and radiated her back with heat. Kurt pulled her into his chest and dropped her to the ground in one swift move as a deafening boom hit her ears.

He thrust one hand in front of them to ease their fall. She cradled her arms around her head. He stayed hunched over her, his forehead touching the ground next to hers. Ripping metal, thuds, glass breaking and crashes surrounded them. She flinched with each sound of impact. Kurt's body lurched sideways. His sudden movement flipped her to her back. He groaned but she was too afraid to open her eyes and look in case stray glass debris hit her. She pressed her hands over her face. Splatters of wet and powdery substances fell onto her hands. It didn't burn, so she prayed nothing landing on them was acidic or toxic.

The air stilled except for the smoke alarms beeping in unison from inside the house and in the garage. She opened her fingers enough to peek. The connecting door to the house was no longer on its hinges but up against the SUV's windshield. Amazingly it had only cracked the glass but hadn't broken it.

Smoke rolled toward them from inside the house. The corners of the garage door bent outward, revealing sunlight and shoes rushing toward them. Tools that had once hung on the pegboard against the wall had impaled the rest of the garage door.

She gulped. If they'd still been standing...

Tears pricked her vision. She turned her head to Kurt. He lay flat on his stomach, half underneath the side of the SUV, covered in brown paint. A can from the garage shelf must have hit him. Her lungs burned, and while the last thing she wanted to do was to talk, she tried anyway. "Are you—" Coughs racked her body and she couldn't say any more.

Kurt propped up on his elbows and nodded. No words came out of his mouth, either, but she took it to mean he was okay. Men shouted outside, their words muffled over the high-pitched ringing in her ears.

The garage door creaked and groaned until the officers had opened it enough to enter. One officer rushed toward her and picked her up by the elbows. Her limbs moved like a rag doll until her sense of up and down returned and she could stand. Kurt waved off the officer helping him, stood and reached for her hand.

Concern lined his features. While the coughs had momentarily ceased, her lungs were still angry, and she didn't trust herself to speak. She squeezed Kurt's hand and tried to smile so he'd know she was okay, but he didn't let go. They made their way to a decorative boulder in the front yard and sat side by side. An ambulance and fire truck rushed down the street toward the property.

She began to shiver even though it wasn't cold. She blinked rapidly. She couldn't believe what had just happened. Had the flowers blown up? Kurt dropped her hand, wrapped his arm around her shoulders and pulled her close. His lungs must've hurt, too, because he still made no effort to talk. His warmth kept her teeth from chattering.

Logically she'd known that someone wanted to kill her. She'd known it from the time they'd escaped the truck underwater. She'd known someone was capable of murder after seeing Levi. But somehow she'd deluded herself into thinking that the truck incident was going to be the worst of it. The bomb meant they were against someone equipped with ingenuity and a brazen determination.

It was time to face the truth. Whoever was behind this wasn't going to stop until she was dead.

Kurt kept a protective arm around Rebecca while the firemen poured out of the emergency vehicle. He didn't trust himself to speak. If he did, words he might regret would be targeted at the officers who'd allowed the vase to pass inspection.

His court security officers would've never allowed something like this to happen. Of course, he'd trained them personally, and they had the ability to scan and x-ray everything that tried to come into the courts. But still. How could the police officers have missed a bomb in the vase unless one of them was in on it?

Rebecca turned into him, her cheek resting against his chest. She'd had faith in him, she'd said. He couldn't help but feel he'd failed her. Yet she didn't act repulsed by him. Maybe it'd hit her later. He'd learned long ago that people only believed in you when you were doing something that benefited them.

She lifted her chin and her eyes met his. A million emotions he couldn't identify unfurled within his chest. "Are you okay?" he asked. He sounded a little like a bullfrog, but the irritation in his throat was lessening with the fresh air.

She blinked slowly. "Yes. Thank you." She coughed again and he patted her back in a poor attempt to help.

"I've been shot at, choked and knifed. Never did I ever imagine I'd be almost taken out by flowers."

EMT workers who looked familiar rushed to their side. Kurt answered a barrage of questions about pain, not able to keep up with the answers Rebecca was giving her respective technician. Their vitals were taken and Rebecca waved away an oxygen mask. "I'll be fine. I think whatever was in that smoke irritated my lungs."

The man in uniform sunk to one knee and handed her a water bottle. "Well, drink this down and then we'll make the call about whether we should give you a ride to the hospital or not."

They handed Kurt his own water bottle, even though, aside from some bruised muscles and brown paint drying on the back of his neck, he felt fine.

"Adrenaline can mask pain," the EMT said. Kurt knew that but didn't reply.

The EMT in front of Rebecca seemed to have eyes only for her. "I may not be in law enforcement, but it seems pretty obvious somebody isn't happy with you."

She gave a small laugh in reply.

His entire body tensed and his blood boiled. Why did everyone need to keep reminding him that he was in law enforcement? He knew already, and he knew that meant he shouldn't let himself have feelings for Rebecca.

"Sir, your heart rate and pressure just spiked. Are you okay?"

Kurt hadn't even realized the EMT sitting next to him had a blood pressure cuff on his right arm. "I'm fine. I need to speak with her alone. Is she cleared?"

Rebecca turned wide eyes on him.

The EMT nodded. "We'll give you a minute and come back and check your vitals again."

"Did you see something?" she asked.

"Do you have a boyfriend?" His voice sounded louder than he intended.

Her eyes narrowed. "Why? Do you have a girl-friend?"

He pursed his lips at the ludicrous question. Why would she even ask? "No, and I would think it was obvious why I need to know. There's a chance we're barking up the wrong tree. Could this be personal? Flowers might indicate—"

"Oh." She bit her lip and shook her head. "Sorry. I'm not thinking clearly yet. No, there's no one. I travel a lot. Nothing ever serious."

"I didn't mean to bark." He blew out a long breath. "For a moment there, I was scared I'd los—"

"Don't say it. You saved my life. Again. That's what matters." She gestured at the firemen pouring out of her grandfather's house. "And stopping whoever did this from trying again."

A fireman pulled off his face mask and pointed at Kurt. "You the deputy marshal?"

Kurt stood and recognized the man as the fire chief. The handlebar moustache was a dead giveaway. "You got something for me?"

"We got the fire out," the chief answered. "My men

are making sure it can't start back up again. You'd be surprised how many times we get called back on a relit. It's a nightmare." He gestured backward. "The structural integrity of the house seems sound. You can thank the vaulted ceilings for that. It had enough force it could've shifted the house off its foundation, but the open layout allowed for dissipation. The kitchen is in pretty bad shape, though, and the living room windows and the main door to the garage were blown off, but all the walls are there."

That was good news for Judge Linn as it likely meant a relatively fast repair and remodel, but it didn't help Kurt get any better an understanding as to what happened. "How does a bomb go unnoticed in a flower vase? I'm assuming that's where it came from."

"Babette!" Rebecca jumped up, her face ashen. "My grandpa owns a cat. Was she—"

A police officer approached, holding the Siamese cat. "Are you looking for this girl?" The man scratched behind Babette's ears. "She's been keeping us company at the gate all day."

"Oh, thank you." Rebecca leaned forward and pulled the wiggling cat into her arms. "I imagine Grandpa will be glad you are a little escape artist now." Babette had likely escaped when Delaney had come around the last time.

Kurt's fist tensed at the sight of the officer who had insisted the flowers were safe.

The man's eyes widened. "I'm telling you, I looked right down in the vase. There was nothing there but water."

The chief held up his thumb and index finger about four inches apart. "It was a small conical device that made this mess. It could've been designed to match the vase. You think you're looking at the bottom of it, but really you're looking at the top of the bomb."

Kurt exhaled. "How would you know that?"

"I found the cap and the threading used in the device. I'm no expert, so don't quote me. I've taken some classes, and we have a SWAT guy that keeps us updated on all the different methods of bomb making." The chief hitched a thumb over his shoulder. "One thing I know for sure. Whoever put that together knew his stuff. ATF is on the way for the investigation."

The Bureau of Alcohol, Tobacco, Firearms and Explosives would be the best choice to answer Kurt's questions, but they'd take too long to reach a conclusion.

The chief leaned forward with conspiratorial posturing. "So when I tell you this is my unofficial opinion, I mean it." He dipped his chin to level his gaze, making sure Kurt understood. "I believe I spotted evidence indicating the bomb had a remote detonator."

Great. Kurt was doing such a bang-up job at protecting Rebecca that all he needed was a homicidal bomb expert to come after them. The judge would love that news. He rounded his back, hunched his shoulders and let his sarcastic thoughts wash over him.

Hating the threat didn't make it go away, though. If someone set it off remotely, then they should be searching the area. He straightened and pointed to the officer. "Tell me you have the driver's license of the floral van."

"Absolutely. Scanned it and the plates when he pulled in."

Finally. Something had gone right. Technology updates had slowed many things down in law enforcement with extra training and glitches that had to be fixed with each upgrade, but the ability to share information in a heartbeat was invaluable. "Text it to me and send the alert out to police and the Sheriff's Office." He rattled off his phone number as the officer tapped rapidly on his own phone.

Kurt received the text and zoomed in on the license. The man looked like the body-builder type. He had a thick neck covered in tattoos and a beard covering his chin. "This is exactly how he looked?"

The officer shifted uncomfortably. "Well, not exactly. He had a ball cap on and said he'd shaved his beard off and lost some weight. But otherwise, he looked pretty similar."

Kurt tried to hold in his groan. While photos could be old and people changed, he didn't feel convinced they weren't looking at a false identification.

"Did he have the same tattoos?"

The officer's face gave him answer. He hadn't noticed. At least the tech guy at the courthouse had done an excellent job duplicating Kurt's previous setup on the new smartphone. The tools he used to check the fugitive database were right where he wanted them. Thirty seconds later he got the "not found" message, which meant the guy wasn't a known fugitive…yet.

"Can I see?" Rebecca leaned over his shoulder, trying to get a good look.

He flinched, hopefully not enough that she noticed. She seemed to be comfortable getting close to him, on a regular basis. "Here, take Babette first." She dumped the cat into his arms before he could even object.

The officers and chief had amused smirks as they

looked between him and Rebecca, as if they knew something he didn't. He wanted to wipe the grins off their ugly mugs. "I hate cats," he mumbled. "You want it back?" he asked the officer.

Rebecca slipped the phone out of his hand. "Oh, but she likes you."

"I've got to get on this APB anyway," the officer said and walked away.

Babette stretched her neck and rubbed her white fur against his chin. It had to be prickly with his five-o'clock shadow. Maybe the cat wanted a scratching post. Or did cats claw a scratching post? His uncertainty was evidence that he didn't care enough to know. "Can I let her down to roam?"

"Too many birds of prey around here," she answered. "I'm thankful she's stayed safe this long."

The chief pointed to the road. "I think the ATF is almost here." He sauntered off with a grin.

Rebecca stretched her fingers over the screen until the man's photo filled the screen. She adjusted her grip until her fingers could cover most everything but his eyes. She shook her head and sighed. "It's not the guy."

Kurt's gut tightened, and the cat responded by purring and curling up into his chest. Rebecca's eyes looked moist as she looked up into the clear sky, marred only by a few coiled tendrils of remaining smoke. "It might've been the guy if he used a fake identification of someone just similar enough to pass it off."

He'd already considered that. The cat had the audacity to fall asleep in his arms. Well, he wasn't having that. "Take her back." He bent over and tried to shift the cat, who seemed to have no intention of waking up, into her arms. His face brushed up against her forehead during the clumsy exchange. His neck heated and the idea of Rebecca curled up against his chest instead proved difficult to forget.

He straightened and took his phone from her. Their fingers brushed and a soft smile crossed her face. Was it possible she was attracted to him? He cleared his throat and turned toward the house. He waved his arm at the expanse of hills and trees on one side of the property. "Whoever did this had plenty of places he could hide and watch to set off the detonator. From there, someone could see us pull in to the garage."

The cat wiggled in her arms and complained vocally with warbling meows. Rebecca ignored her. "The bomb went off maybe a minute and a half after we pulled in to the garage."

"Exactly. Someone waited until they thought we would be inside." The bomber's plan had nearly worked.

A white SUV with dark-tinted windows drove down the street. While he couldn't be certain until it got closer, it was probably Delaney. The vehicle in the garage couldn't be driven until the windshield was repaired and the rest inspected. It was designed to handle gunshots, so hopefully it would be roadworthy soon. For now, they'd have to rely on Delaney as their ride. Even though she was a newbie, she'd had the smarts to add darkened windows to her personal vehicle.

The window rolled down at the gate and the officers waved the vehicle inside. Sure enough, Delaney pulled up right next to them. "At this rate we'll have to be borrowing CSO cars." She tossed Kurt her keys. "You can drive mine for now. The Spokane office is considering sending us reinforcements."

It was about time. "And the hesitation?"

"Whether it's deemed a true threat to the court."

He gritted his teeth. "What do they call a bomb in the judge's house? Sounds credible to me."

Delaney's eyes flicked to Rebecca, who acted as if she wasn't listening while she petted Babette. "They're reviewing the case and the judge's request. There's some question as to whether it would've happened at all if the judge was here, or if his granddaughter was in Ohio." Her voice remained low, but Kurt felt certain by the way Rebecca sucked in a sharp breath that she'd still heard. Delaney held up a hand. "What if we called the county's victim-witness coordinator?"

And she'd just proved the reason Judge Linn had requested him. A newbie had yet to learn all the ins and outs of interagency cooperation. "Their hands are tied unless a felony has already been filed."

She sighed. "Okay. I'll stay and run point here," Delaney said in a much stronger voice. "Your new base is at the motel. Rooms are already set up. I'll come by, as soon as I have another vehicle, with clothes for you, Rebecca. That'll give Kurt a chance to gather his clothes."

He pointed at the cat. "Pretty sure they don't allow animals."

"That's okay," Rebecca said. "We can drop her off at the vet. I know for a fact they'll spoil her rotten in boarding. They've nicknamed her the Queen B."

She might envy the cat when she saw where they

were going, then. Sometimes staying safe on a government budget meant discomfort. He hoped it would be worth it.

SEVEN

Rebecca stared at her grandfather's property fading into the distance as they rounded the curved road. "Some of my best childhood memories were at that house before Dad got too nervous about us visiting." She pointed at the steep hill that led to the lake. "The house used to have a rail system. My parents were on an anniversary getaway and—" she smiled at the memory "—Grandma let us climb into the tram to ride down to the dock to the speedboat they used to own. Mom and Dad showed up as we were heading down, arms in the air, like it was a roller coaster."

"There aren't very many of those left in the area, but the ones I've seen don't go very fast at all."

"No, but neither does the Small World ride at Disneyland. As a kid, I might as well have been on a dragon, I thought it was so cool."

"Your grandma sounds like a spitfire."

"She was."

"So you took after her."

She felt her eyebrows jump. Had she? Her grandma was fearless, fiercely committed, and supportive of Grandpa and his work. She glanced at Kurt's profile. Could she ever be like that? Delaney's words ran through her head. She bit her lip and blurted, "Maybe it would be better for everyone if I got back to Ohio."

"That's a bad idea." Kurt's voice rose. "If you leave now, I can't guarantee your safety. I'd be hard-pressed to get you round-the-clock protection from the Marshals if they conclude the threat isn't against the court."

"Isn't that what we're all thinking? It must be linked to Vista Resort Properties. So when you agree with the rest of them, I'll lose your protection, as well."

He shook his head. "I won't accept that. It may be a gray area, but I can choose to accept the judge's request to guard you. Whoever is out there isn't only a threat to you but society. And for all we know, he'll target the judge to get to you. So don't worry about protection. I'm not backing down until I'm convinced you're safe."

She leaned back and admired his passion for his work. That's all it was, a drive to make sure he did a job well done. Still, her heart warmed from his words. Despite the danger, she felt physically safe with him by her side. Her heart was another matter.

It was time to get logical. If she went back to Ohio, her firm would only send another auditor to the valley to make sure the truth was uncovered. Whoever followed her footsteps wouldn't have a judge as a relative who could ask for special protection. *Right, Lord? I want Your wisdom but need You to make it abundantly clear.*

The police chief might be willing to offer protection if they had enough evidence of foul play. How likely was it they could keep another auditor safe when they'd allowed a bomb to go right past them? To be fair, it sounded like even the marshals wouldn't have spotted it. What kind of person knew how to do such things? How were they ever going to win against someone like that?

Babette squirmed in her arms, trying her best to jump up onto Kurt's arm that rested on the console. She'd seen Babette try hard to get close to Grandpa in the same way. She'd read that cats could be good judges of character. Some cats also seemed to zero in on emotions and especially feel drawn to someone who needs love and affection. Were Grandpa and Kurt both in more need of comfort than she was?

She gave him directions on how to get to the vet, and it took only a few minutes to run Babette in to the welcoming staff. "We have something to show you when you come back," the technician hollered after her. Rebecca didn't have time to look at new collars. Babette wasn't even her cat. She waved her thanks and joined Kurt, who was waiting at the front door, ever alert.

He drove through the main portion of Coeur d'Alene with its cute specialty shops the tourists and locals alike loved, including All Things Irish, Christmas at the Lake and Mrs. Honeypeeps Sweet Shop. She leaned forward. "Maybe we should stop at Exclusively Wigs and Things. If no one can recognize me, maybe the danger will stop."

He gave her a side glance. "I hate it to break it to you, but a wig isn't going to make people forget you."

"What is that supposed to mean?"

His neck reddened and his lips pressed together to make a firm line. He kept his eyes firmly on the road. "Some people," he said very slowly, "are memorable once you see their face. It wouldn't matter what their hair looked like because they're different enough that you could spot them out of a crowd by their eyes or their smile or something."

Reading between the lines, she wondered if he was trying to say she was pretty or the opposite. "Does that observation warrant a thank-you?"

He barked a laugh and his shoulders relaxed. "It was a compliment. But, moving on, we need to get to our safe location to plan the next move."

"I hate planning."

"Why?"

"I prefer to live in the moment."

"We share that in common, but that doesn't negate planning."

She held her hand out as if it was going to chop something. "You look at the facts and make a choice. Boom. No plan needed. Contingencies just take extra time when there isn't any reason. Grandma liked to quote Bible verses all the time. And she had one hanging up that said planning and boasting about what you're going to do today or tomorrow is useless when you have no idea what tomorrow will bring."

Kurt scratched his chin as if the stubble starting to appear was bothering him. The five-o'clock shadow looked good on him. "I know that one," he said. "But it doesn't say plans are bad, it's saying it's foolish to be concrete and arrogant about your plans. The point is to be sensitive to what the Lord has in store for you. Even the apostles planned. I could be wrong, but I think Proverbs calls people who don't prepare sluggards."

For some reason it didn't feel awkward to discuss scriptures with him, but he seemed to appreciate healthy discussion. He proved to be an intelligent man, versed in many subjects. She wondered if he was a believer, as well, but knowing some scriptures didn't necessarily mean anything.

The storefronts, houses and landscaping morphed into barbed-wire fences and fields, some littered with old cars slated for junkyards. What motel could be this far on the outskirts of town? There would be absolutely no view of the lake the way the road curved. "You had plans go wrong before, right? When even contingencies didn't work?"

"Sure. So, I evaluated my choices and made new plans. Are you telling me you didn't have any plans? How'd you end up as an accountant?"

She shrugged. "My dad's research found it was the safest career, both monetarily and dangerwise."

"But then you took a position that took you everywhere around the country." He laughed. "I'll take a guess that wasn't what he imagined for you."

Fair point, but she didn't comment on that aspect. "It's not as glamorous as it sounds. I see the insides of hotels, cubicles and conference rooms more than the adventures I imagined." She shook her head. How'd he turn the conversation back to her? "The point is that sitting and talking about what you might and might not do does nothing. Like now, for instance. You're saying it's not the best idea to go to Ohio. Fine. I'll agree to that, but then what am I supposed to do? I think we should turn around and go back to the corporate offices right now. Make something happen."

"I prefer action, too, Rebecca." He glanced at her. "But you're wrong about one thing. We're not sitting around. We're making sure you're safe and regrouping so that we can make a smart next step."

She slumped into her seat. "Hear me out. We go back to the offices. This time, you flash your badge. I'm sure we could get in and find the missing link. It has to point to whoever killed Levi and targeted me."

"Believe it or not, I've already been thinking about it. But we need to do it the right way. It's clear they don't want you there anymore, or the CEO would've called you back."

"Yeah, that's suspicious."

"We need a warrant." He flipped on his blinker.

They passed one more tree and he turned into a small driveway that led to a dilapidated pink building. Six doors and six windows lined the front with a vending machine, which looked as if it hadn't been stocked in years, in the middle. A pool, barely bigger than a hot tub, covered in a thick layer of mildewed leaves, sat to the right of the parking lot. She gulped. "Well, I can guarantee no one would ever think of looking for me here."

He glanced at her apologetically. "Delaney booked us two rooms. I'll stay with you in the day, and she'll stay in your room with you at night while I'm next door. There are no connecting rooms, unfortunately."

It had to be the cheapest motel in the entire tristate area. And if the rooms looked anything like the outside, she might let Delaney sleep while she kept a lookout. She'd done all-nighters all the time in college and survived by taking naps during the day. She could do it again, though now, if she stayed up past midnight, she got nauseous from being overtired, a lovely byproduct of growing up. "What if I chipped in some extra money so we could stay somewhere a little nicer?"

He shifted the SUV into Park directly in front of the motel office. "Money isn't the issue." He shook his head. "Okay, it's part of the issue, but the point is that we're out of the way and in a clearing. The Sheriff's Office is only two more minutes down the road for backup. Stay here, and I'll grab the keys."

"No one but Delaney knows we're here. Can I stay with you?" She bit her lip and hated to admit that after the day she'd had she was scared to be left alone.

His forehead creased for a moment. "Fine." He hopped out of the vehicle and let her out. She didn't need his hand, but she took it anyway, and the warmth traveled up her arm yet again. A girl could get used to that. She followed him into the office.

A tall man wore soundproof headphones while he moved his head back and forth in rhythm. His head was barely visible over the cheap countertop desk so she couldn't see what he was doing. Kurt held a hand out and peeked his head over.

The man jolted. His entire body shook so hard his headphones slipped off this head and he reared back. "Man, don't sneak up on someone like that." He stood and held a hand over his heart. "I was at the end of a level." He glanced at Rebecca and did a double take. "Hey, don't I know you?"

Kurt's frown deepened. "I doubt it. She's from out of town."

If he recognized her, did that mean the media had picked up the story? Except his tall, gangly appearance seemed familiar to her, as well. His name tag was crooked on the red polo he wore. "Elijah Holmes?"

"Yeah, you remember me!"

Actually she knew it from his name tag, but she did remember that they'd gone to summer camp once together back when her dad had let her visit in the summers. He'd been a gangly boy back then, as well, and had told everyone he was related to Sherlock Holmes.

She reached over the countertop and gave him a half hug before straightening. "Great to see you. How are you?"

"Well, I got fired from the resort and I'm working here, so you figure it out. Checking in?"

Ah. Kurt's neck had returned to the red hue she'd grown accustomed to, only this time she could see the strong muscles and tendons surrounding it. Kurt held up a hand. "Excuse us for a moment, Elijah."

He raised his eyebrows. "Do we know each other, too?"

Kurt raised an eyebrow. "I just heard her use your name, and it's on your shirt." He put a hand on Rebecca's back and led her outside to the sidewalk. "We can't stay here."

She pumped her fist in mock celebration. "Yes. Can I ask why? Is it because he recognized me?" She shook her head. "Never mind. I don't need to know. I'm not arguing. Let's go."

His lips moved to one side. "That's a first."

She playfully smacked his side. "It's called having an opinion."

"Elijah knows who you are and has seen you. We can't trust he won't let it leak to the wrong person." He led her to the SUV and opened the door. "So you know each other?"

She hopped in and reached for the inside handle, but

Kurt made no movement to leave. "We were friends. We went to summer camp together once. Decades ago. I remembered him because of his unusual name."

"Doesn't seem that unusual to me."

"It was his last name. Reminded me of Sherlock, and I was really into mysteries back then."

"You hung out together?"

"Well, no. But we were both there."

"See? A wig wouldn't help. You're very memorable. How many years ago was that anyway?"

"I'd rather not think about just how many years. It was in junior high, though."

His lips curved. "You weren't friends. By your description, I'd hardly even call it acquaintances."

"Does that matter?"

"Not today." He closed the door and walked around the SUV, leaving her wondering what he meant.

Maybe she hugged people often and considered everyone "friends." Even the kind she'd met only once that should really be called acquaintances. It shouldn't bother him. He wasn't jealous of the guy. Her tendency toward outward affection meant that the way she'd curled up against him earlier probably hadn't meant anything.

Rebecca was a people person, a trait he admired but didn't share or fully understand. Those types were often mistaken for flirts when, really, they were just being friendly. He exhaled and opened his side of the vehicle.

"Did I do something to offend you?"

Kurt should've known to rein in his last little comment. The woman would address any issue head-on, except of course, her family's rule about fraternizing with law enforcement. He could probably gather statistics to show that she'd actually be safer if she had a relationship with someone in his line of work. Not that he had any motivation to do so. "I'm annoyed with the situation."

She crossed her arms. "And not with me?"

He had no reason to be upset with her. So why wouldn't that nagging feeling go away? The answer came immediately. He wanted her to like him, to be falling for him. Add it to the long list of frustrations. God could've chosen to keep him from breaking his ankle—a moment that forever changed the way his friends and father viewed him—and ruining his chances at a scholarship and professional baseball. He believed and trusted in Him but sometimes wondered if the big guy upstairs was disappointed with him. Or maybe it was the other way around, something he wasn't ready to admit.

"Where to next?" she asked.

That was the question of the day. "I guess I can take you to my home, only until we can arrange other accommodations for the night."

"Good. I'll get to learn about the man behind the badge."

She really needed to stop looking at people with adoring hazel eyes. "What you see is what you get."

Her smile faded. "Of course."

His phone buzzed. "Deputy Marshal Brock."

"Detective Hall from the Sheriff's Office."

"Detective, I'm really hoping you have some good news to share."

"Unfortunately there are no spreadsheets or financial documents to be found on Mr. Garner's cloud account."

Kurt hit the steering wheel with the palm of his hand. *Why couldn't at least one thing go right, Lord? It's not as if You can't make it happen.* Kurt knew God wasn't a butler in the sky waiting to take his orders, but he didn't understand why things were so hard to accomplish that seemed like they should be squarely in His will.

In his periphery, Rebecca leaned over, trying to get his attention. She had her eyebrows raised and he noticed the question in her eyes. Kurt gave a small shake of the head. Her face fell and her shoulders drooped.

The interchange alone sent him for a loop. He never communicated with someone with such little effort and yet they'd understood each other. It didn't matter, though. No time to reflect on his newfound expertise in body language. "So we're back to square one. No leads," Kurt replied into the phone.

"On the contrary. Tell Miss Linn her hunch was right on the money. There was pertinent information on the gaming console. We accessed an app that contained Levi Garner's personal email account. He sent an email a few days ago to his sister, who apparently was also his real-estate agent. I can send you the email now. I'm wondering if this gives Miss Linn clarity on what happened."

Kurt pulled over to the side of the road as his phone vibrated. "I'll call you back as soon as I have her read it."

He tapped until the email produced the file in question. Rebecca unbuckled her seat belt and leaned over, unwilling to wait for him to read it first before he passed it on.

...shady stuff going on. Found something that to the untrained eye wouldn't mean a thing. I did the math, though, and it's bad. It's probably my imagination, but I think they're watching me. I might not be able to wait to sell the land before I get out of here. I think it'd be best to go off the grid for a bit. What do I need to do to leave the property in your hands?

Rebecca's eyes were wide and her hand covered her mouth. Kurt scrolled down to see the sister's answer.

Can't you take what you saw to the police? You can give me limited power of attorney, specifically to sell the house and land. I do have an investor chomping at the bit to build a few luxury houses there. Levi, should I be worried?

Kurt scrolled to the final email, dated the same day they'd been pushed off the bridge.

Start the paperwork. I'll be by later tonight to sign it on my way out of town. I'm a relative newbie in this town compared to you. I don't think people know we're siblings since we have different last names. Keep it that way.

Her eyes searched his face as she worried her lip. "I feel like I just read a dead man's diary."

"Detective Hall hopes it will give you some insight as to what we are looking for."

She closed her eyes. "I remember a couple of the numbers. They were in the millions and they'd been diverted…" She squeezed her eyes closed tighter and finally exhaled. "I can't remember more." She looked at him and pointed a finger. "If I could just copy their files again into the cloud, I'm sure I could find what I missed the first time."

"That's what I wanted to hear." He called Detective Hall and relayed the message. "So is it enough to get a warrant?" Kurt certainly thought so, but he wasn't in the habit of asking for one locally.

"I was already working on it. I've got a call into the county judge. We can have a warrant in ten minutes, but it's almost closing time at the resort offices and I can't get a full team out there for at least an hour. So I'll plan on going in first thing in the morning."

"Time is of the essence. Whoever is behind this could be getting rid of the numbers Levi found." Kurt didn't wait for Hall to ask. He spun his free hand around the steering wheel until they were heading the opposite direction. "I can get inside and stall until you arrive with the warrant. Send who you can."

"Um…"

"The US Marshals can support local law enforcement and assist with any violent crimes or felons. We're often called upon for surveillance and investigations. It'll still be your case." While true, the US Attorney General was usually the one to assign such tasks. "I'll get my accountant started on locating what we need until you can get an analyst on your team."

He grunted. "Fair enough. I'll text you the warrant as soon as I get it and meet you there."

It had almost been too easy. Kurt half expected a

"4 for 4" MINI-SURVEY

We are prepared to **REWARD** you with 2 FREE books and 2 FREE gifts for completing our MINI SURVEY!

FREE
Value Over
$20!

You'll get...

TWO FREE BOOKS &
TWO FREE GIFTS

just for participating in our Mini Survey!

Dear Reader,

IT'S A FACT: if you answer 4 quick questions, we'll send you **4 FREE REWARDS!**

I'm not kidding you. As a leading publisher of women's fiction, we value your opinions… and your time. That's why we are prepared to **reward** you handsomely for completing our mini-survey. In fact, we have 4 Free Rewards for you, including 2 free books and 2 free gifts.

As you may have guessed, that's why our mini-survey is called **"4 for 4".** Answer 4 questions and get 4 Free Rewards. It's that simple!

Thank you for participating in our survey,

Pam Powers

To get your 4 FREE REWARDS:
Complete the survey below and return the insert today to receive 2 FREE BOOKS and 2 FREE GIFTS guaranteed!

► DETACH AND MAIL CARD TODAY! ►

"4 for 4" MINI-SURVEY

1 Is reading one of your favorite hobbies?
☐ YES ☐ NO

2 Do you prefer to read instead of watch TV?
☐ YES ☐ NO

3 Do you read newspapers and magazines?
☐ YES ☐ NO

4 Do you enjoy trying new book series with FREE BOOKS?
☐ YES ☐ NO

YES! I have completed the above Mini-Survey. Please send me my 4 FREE REWARDS (worth over $20 retail). I understand that I am under no obligation to buy anything, as explained on the back of this card.

❏ I prefer the regular-print edition
153/353 IDL GMYM

❏ I prefer the larger-print edition
107/307 IDL GMYM

FIRST NAME	LAST NAME

ADDRESS

APT.#	CITY

STATE/PROV.	ZIP/POSTAL CODE

Offer limited to one per household and not applicable to series that subscriber is currently receiving.
Your Privacy—The Reader Service is committed to protecting your privacy. Our Privacy Policy is available online at www.ReaderService.com or upon request from the Reader Service. We make a portion of our mailing list available to reputable third parties that offer products we believe may interest you. If you prefer that we not exchange your name with third parties, or if you wish to clarify or modify your communication preferences, please visit us at www.ReaderService.com/consumerschoice or write to us at Reader Service Preference Service, P.O. Box 9062, Buffalo, NY 14240-9062. Include your complete name and address.

SLI-218-MS17

© 2017 HARLEQUIN ENTERPRISES LIMITED
® and ™ are trademarks owned and used by the trademark owner and/or its licensee. Printed in the U.S.A.

READER SERVICE—Here's how it works:

Accepting your 2 free Love Inspired® Suspense books and 2 free gifts (gifts valued at approximately $10.00 retail) places you under no obligation to buy anything. You may keep the books and gifts and return the shipping statement marked "cancel." If you do not cancel, about a month later we'll send you 6 additional books and bill you just $5.24 each for the regular-print edition or $5.74 each for the larger-print edition in the U.S. or $5.74 each for the regular-print edition or $6.24 each for the larger-print edition in Canada. That is a savings of at least 13% off the cover price. It's quite a bargain! Shipping and handling is just 50¢ per book in the U.S. and 75¢ per book in Canada*. You may cancel at any time, but if you choose to continue, every month we'll send you 6 more books, which you may either purchase at the discount price plus shipping and handling or return to us and cancel your subscription. *Terms and prices subject to change without notice. Prices do not include applicable taxes. Sales tax applicable in N.Y. Canadian residents will be charged applicable taxes. Offer not valid in Quebec. Books received may not be as shown. All orders subject to approval. Credit or debit balances in a customer's account(s) may be offset by any other outstanding balance owed by or to the customer. Please allow 4 to 6 weeks for delivery. Offer available while quantities last.

► If offer card is missing write to: Reader Service, P.O. Box 1341, Buffalo, NY 14240-8531 or visit www.ReaderService.com ►

BUSINESS REPLY MAIL
FIRST-CLASS MAIL   PERMIT NO. 717   BUFFALO, NY

POSTAGE WILL BE PAID BY ADDRESSEE

READER SERVICE
PO BOX 1341
BUFFALO NY 14240-8571

NO POSTAGE
NECESSARY
IF MAILED
IN THE
UNITED STATES

fight. He'd never used his privileges before in this way. Ever. But he had multiple arguments prepared if his supervisors received a complaint. By then, Rebecca and Judge Linn should be safely in their respective homes and back to work. His chances at a promotion any time soon might be limited, but he could be alone again, working fugitive cases without someone by his side who insisted on being treated like a partner.

"What was that? Am I your accountant? A consultant?"

"We've got a chance to finish this once and for all." And as far as he was concerned, it couldn't happen fast enough. They had no safe lodging arranged, his right ear still had a ringing in it that was starting to concern him and he was tired. The bone-deep exhaustion was probably the reason he struggled to keep his growing feelings for Rebecca in check. It was too much to handle right now.

"They close at five."

"Then hold on." Kurt pressed the accelerator and since Delaney's car wasn't equipped with lights or sirens, took every back road possible to get him to the corporate offices in record time.

"Am I rubbing off on you?"

"What do you mean?"

"Well, I heard a little of what was said, and you're still covered in paint."

He'd forgotten that little tidbit. The moment he thought about it, he felt the paint cracking on the back of his neck. The adrenaline had kept the discomfort at bay until now.

Rebecca clung to the handle with both hands. "I'm

not arguing with you. I think it's the right call. I just thought you liked plans."

"We've got five minutes to plan. That's all the time in the world."

"Good, because I've been rethinking the strategy. How about we play my auditor card before forcing their hand with the warrant business?"

Kurt could see the pros and cons of both ideas. "Hold that thought." He called Delaney and continued to drive with one hand on the steering wheel. As soon as she answered, he filled her in on the situation. "We're going in, grabbing the numbers and leaving. I need you to pick up Rebecca's laptop from the IT guy and meet me at Vista."

She was silent for a moment.

"Delaney?"

"I don't like it, but you're running this rodeo. Weapons are in the hidden compartment in the trunk of my SUV." She rattled off her gun safe code.

"I don't think I'll be needing that. Police will be coming as backup. Besides, I think we're dealing with a contracted hit."

"Agreed. There's probably no danger within the offices, but it feels rushed."

"The faster we finish this the better." Kurt pulled into the parking lot and glanced down at his clothes. At least most of the paint was on his back, so hopefully it wouldn't be as obvious when he walked inside. "Let's go."

She hopped out of the SUV and joined him on the sidewalk. Only when they were almost to the front door did he realize he had forgotten to tell her to stay put while he looked around for threats before letting her out of the vehicle. He was starting to treat her like a partner and that bothered him. Maybe his judgment was slipping. He faltered at the front door but Rebecca charged ahead into the lobby. She waved at the security guard, the same guy she chatted with the last time they'd entered.

Kurt increased his stride until he was by her side. The CEO, Jake Putnam, was in the lobby with a briefcase, as if he was leaving for the day. "Rebecca. I didn't expect to see you here."

"I really need to finish that audit, Mr. Putnam. It will only take me a moment to get what I need."

He crossed his arms over his chest. "I thought I was going to give you a call."

The auditor strategy wasn't going to work. It was clear Putnam wasn't going to budge. "That was before we found your accountant murdered," Kurt said.

Putnam's face lost all of its color. "What?"

Kurt knew what to look for in liars and this man appeared genuinely shocked. He flashed his badge before Rebecca could say any more. He'd let her speak first only because he was going to let her try out the auditor card, but he didn't agree with the antagonistic approach in this situation. "Deputy Marshal Kurt Brock. A warrant has been issued to search the financial records of Vista Resort Properties."

"Kurt?" Rebecca asked.

He held up one finger as he finished explaining to a quivering Mr. Putnam why they had probable cause and what the warrant would allow him to search. He wasn't required to show the warrant unless he asked, and so far, Mr. Putnam looked unsteady on his feet. "Sir, do you understand wh—"

The man's eyes rolled and the briefcase dropped from his hand as his body went limp. Kurt lunged and caught Mr. Putnam's head and neck before they hit the marble tiles. Well, he hadn't been expecting the man to faint. "Rebecca—" Kurt looked up to find an empty lobby.

Rebecca was gone.

EIGHT

Rebecca walked alongside the security guard with the name tag S. Howard in the hallway, right next to the lobby. She could still see Kurt, so she wasn't really worried. The guard had approached her while Kurt was talking and asked if she needed anything before he went off duty. "Yes, actually. I'm wondering if there's surveillance footage of the accounting department." If she could confirm her suspicions that Levi had slipped her the flash drive, she could also see what Levi had been doing moments before that. Maybe it would give her clues as to where to start looking. And Kurt would be impressed at her efficiency.

"My boss mans the security camera feeds." Mr. Howard pointed ahead. "I think we archive our camera footage, but I haven't been trained on all of that. Come to think of it, I'm not sure if we have cameras in Accounting. Follow me and you can ask the head of security for yourself. It's just ahead."

If it was just ahead it had to be in one of the side rooms off the hallway, so if Kurt ever looked up, she could wave him down and they could go in together. Perfectly safe. They were in a brightly lit office building, and the security guard served as protection. Besides, Kurt had referred to her as *his accountant* to the detective. The police and the Marshals needed her help. It was a heady feeling, especially given her early childhood dreams, and she felt determined not to let them down. It might prove something to both her grandpa and dad if she played a part in bringing her attacker to justice.

Except they passed four doors. And any minute now, she wouldn't have a visual on Kurt. "Maybe I should go back first and let the marshal know."

He stopped at one of the potted plants and swiveled, one hand on a flashlight attached to his belt. Actually, besides his phone, it was the only tool on his belt. "That's up to you, but I heard the jingling of his keys. He's probably just around the corner. Hey, did you go to Figpickels?"

"What?"

"The toy store, Figpickels. You're bound to find a fun souvenir there for your niece. Otherwise, Souvenir and Sundry has this cute moose straw— Oh here we are."

She'd forgotten they had discussed souvenirs earlier in the week. They turned a corner into a darkened hallway. Her footsteps faltered. She hadn't meant to go this far. The jingling of keys he'd mentioned cued her to another person approaching before she could see the silhouetted form walk closer.

"Sir, I'm checking out for the night," the guard said. "This lady is with the US marshal up front and has a question for you." He nodded at Rebecca and pressed on a swinging door. "Nice to meet you. Have a good night." He looked up briefly. "Weird. Usually this hall-way is lit. Want me to report it before I leave?"

"No. I'll do it. Have a good night."

She heard the hint of an accent. Rebecca stayed where she was since there was light still coming from the other hallway around the corner. The guard stepped into the light, and his eyes looked stone cold.

Her throat tightened. She knew those eyes. Her heart pounded against her ribs. It was the guy—the attacker—standing right in front of her at arm's length.

"You have a question?"

Her breath grew shallow. If he was trying to play like he didn't know her, then maybe she could play along and pretend she didn't recognize him, either. It seemed like the best option in the hope she could get out of there alive.

"Yes, yes, I was going to ask something." She took a step backward, closer to the lighted hallway. Her question was just out of grasp, but she had a hard time remembering as her mind played an insistent loop of: *Run. Run now. Why aren't you running?*

He stepped closer. The patience in his eyes dimmed. She took a deep breath and could run but there wasn't anything between him and her. "I was just wonder-ing if there's security footage of the accounting de-partment."

He pursed his lips and narrowed his eyes. "Yes. I believe so. Follow me, I'm glad to show you." He waved her toward the dark part of the hall. What kind of security guard wouldn't ask her who she was? And why weren't the lights on in this hall? He didn't even challenge her right to watch the security footage. That confirmed her suspicion.

The other guard had said his boss manned the feeds, which meant he'd probably seen them coming. So there could be only one reason for the darkness. He wanted to get her farther away from other people.

Instead she took a step backward and bumped into one of the corner planters with the silk plants. "That's great. Let me just get my—"

He pulled a gun from behind his back. "Okay, no more games." His accent was unmistakable now. Her dad had always told her that if someone pointed a gun at her she was to remain calm—easier said than done—and look the person in the eyes to make sure they remembered you were human. Apparently that reminder was supposed to make some shooters uncomfortable.

She forced her gaze to look straight into the man's eyes. He didn't flinch or blink. Instead he smiled and stepped closer. Great. It didn't work on him. "I'm not playing games," she said. Her voice shook despite her bravado. "I'm not a big fan of guns pointed at me, so if you'll excuse me…"

"No." His entire body blocked her path, the back of her legs pressed up against the planter, and he pointed the gun at her chest. With his free hand he touched her hair. "I admire strong women. I didn't want to kill you, *preciosa*."

She flinched at his touch, but if he admired that she was a strong woman, she had to keep from falling apart. She didn't know Spanish well, but it seemed like he'd called her precious. "So don't."

His hand moved down to her left arm. Her stomach flipped with nausea. If she screamed now, would he shoot her before Kurt could get there to help? His grip tightened and his eyes narrowed. "You wouldn't drop it. You kept looking. Now it's out of my hands. Come with me."

"See, that's where I think you're wrong. You're holding the gun, so it seems like it is in your hands and I'll be glad to drop it. Won't pick it up ever again."

He squeezed her hand so hard she cried out. She leaned away from him. Her other fingertips brushed up against the leaves.

"You scream and your friend dies, too."

He let up on his grip just enough, her fingers scooped up a handful of white rocks. "Okay," she said softly. Then she flung the rocks into his face.

He cursed and the hand with the gun moved up to his face, but he didn't let go of her arm. She grabbed another rock and pressed it into the place she thought she'd scratched him with the letter opener. He bellowed and finally released her, but she was still pinned between him, the wall and the planter.

She pulled her knee up, but only grazed his legs. Her hands fisted and torpedoed his torso, but it was like hitting a hard piece of furniture. The man only took half a step back, but it was enough to squeeze around the planter. She sprinted around the hallway corner.

Crack!

A scream tore from her throat as plaster from the wall where she'd been only half a second ago exploded. Her shaking fingers couldn't decide whether to cover her ears or head, so she ran with her hands in the air.

A silhouette appeared at the end of the hallway. She flinched and threw herself against the wall. She was surrounded.

"Get down!"

She recognized the voice. Kurt. She looked over her shoulder to find the security guard raising his weapon. Rebecca slid down to the ground. Kurt readied his stance, pointed his weapon and yelled, "Stop!"

The guard swiveled. The sound of his retreating footsteps and a door slamming echoed through the empty corridors. Kurt sprinted toward her, gun in hand. "Is that the guy?"

"Yes." Her voice shook. "It's him."

"Then I'm taking the shot next time," he shouted as he ran past her and another door slammed.

Rebecca dropped her head into her hands. What had just happened? She was talking to a friendly security guard who she was sure wasn't a threat. She'd felt safe with him. It never occurred to her that the threat could be waiting around the corner. She'd fully expected it be from someone more invested in the company, like Mr. Putnam, who had contracted a hit.

"Miss Linn?"

Rebecca looked up to see Delaney approaching fast, her hand on her holster. "Are you okay?"

"Y-yes. I'm fine."

"Where's the marshal?"

"He took off after the head of security. He's the one that attacked me that night."

Delaney removed a cell phone from her belt and spoke tersely. She hung up and took a knee. "The police had just arrived. They're securing the building. An ambulance is on the way for Mr. Putnam. I'm going to want them to check you out just in case."

"Mr. Putnam? What happened to him?"

"I'm sure Deputy Marshal Brock is the best person to ask. Putnam's secretary seems to think it was his fault." Delaney offered a hand. "Can you walk? I'd like to get you back in the lobby. I don't like that darkened hallway. Looks like they really shut down this place at quitting time."

"I think he turned off those lights on purpose. The other guard, the good one, he seemed to think it was weird it was off." Rebecca put a hand on the wall to give herself a push as she took Delaney's assistance with the other hand.

"We'll still need to question him, the other guard. He might've led you there as an accomplice."

Rebecca hated to think that. She really did like his advice on the moose straw because he was right that Mandy would love it. In fact, by the looks of her home screen, Mandy had been trying to text her for the past several days. It was unlike Rebecca not to be sending funny selfies and playing online games with her while out of town.

They reached the lobby at the same time as the paramedics. The one on the right gave her a glance and shook his head in mock disgust. "If I'm here for you again…"

"Not me. I'm fine." The paramedic continued on to Mr. Putnam, who was seated with his head between his knees.

Delaney gave her a side glance. "I thought we agreed to getting you checked out."

"I don't remember agreeing. He didn't hurt me."

She raised an eyebrow. "Were you always this stubborn or is the marshal a bad influence?" She shook her head. "Forget I said that."

The frustration was evident in the young woman's

question. She'd never imagined that Delaney and Kurt had any personal relationship, but the annoyance made Rebecca wonder. "I'm afraid I come by a strong-headed streak naturally."

"Well, are you going to do something about this?" The secretary's shrill voice was directed at Delaney.

Detective Hall gave Rebecca a weary glance before addressing the secretary. "Can you tell me what you saw?"

"The marshal spoke to Mr. Putnam and—" The secretary waved behind her. "Well, see for yourself. He went down like a ton of bricks. I'm sure he hit him."

"You saw the marshal use force?"

"No, but—"

"I fainted, Paula," Mr. Putnam groaned, his head between his legs. "I'm not proud of it, but he didn't hit me." He looked up as the paramedic grabbed his wrist to take his vitals. His eyes darted Rebecca's way. "Please tell your grandpa I didn't know anything about this. He's never going to talk to me again."

"What's that mean?" Delaney muttered.

Rebecca had no idea, but she knew Putnam played golf with her grandpa most weekends during the spring and summer. She stepped closer as the paramedic tried to get the man to look into the penlight. "What didn't you know?"

"About the danger. I never would've agreed to hire you if I'd known. You have to tell him. Please."

Putnam never would've agreed to hire her? That didn't make sense. She'd volunteered for the assignment when she'd heard it was in Coeur d'Alene. Or, at least, that's what her supervisor made her believe.

"Did you specifically request me when you contacted my auditing firm?"

Genuine surprise creased his forehead. "Your grandpa wanted to invest here, in Vista Resort Properties. He said he would only do it if you audited it, though. I thought you knew."

Her stomach heated. Why would Grandpa do that and not tell her? It was good practice for an investor to have a third-party audit first, and doubly important for a federal judge. Their investments became public record to prevent presiding certain cases that could result in conflicts of interest. Even if it wasn't required, Grandpa was all about accountability and integrity. Though, it didn't seem very honest that he'd never told Rebecca he'd requested her.

"That's an interesting tidbit the judge failed to mention." Delaney looked over her shoulder. "What happened, Kurt?"

Rebecca followed her gaze. Kurt had holstered his weapon and was striding toward them. He ignored Delaney, though, and made a beeline for Rebecca. "Are you okay? Why did you run off like that?" His eyes searched hers as if he didn't believe she was really okay.

"I didn't run off. I tried to get your attention, but the security guard was talking to me. I never intended to go out of your sight." It struck her now as impulsive. If one guard was leaving, another one was probably coming on duty. Maybe the head of security took over at that point, and if she'd just waited, then she could've figured out his identity with the light of all the lobby windows and pointed him out discreetly to Kurt. Of course, if she'd done that, then it was possible

Mr. Putnam and the secretary would've been caught in gun crossfire. Someone could've been killed. She straightened her shoulders, more confident that she'd done nothing wrong. "I got away, and you made sure he didn't catch me. He works here, so we can find out his identity and hunt him down now."

Delaney cleared her throat. "Kurt? Could I have a word?"

Rebecca had a feeling they were both in trouble.

Kurt walked over to the side of the room, barely out of earshot from the paramedics, the police and Rebecca. His heart still pounded in his throat from the intense run after the security guard. There was no way the supposed guard didn't have military training. He'd scaled a landscape wall in the back of the building and run into the trees. Two minutes later, Kurt had heard the sound of a motor and abandoned his pursuit.

Delaney's mouth and eyes held hints of strain. She placed her hands on her hips as if ready to abandon her usual calm.

"Now, before you say anything, I know I should've never let Rebecca out of my sight in the first place. It was a rookie mistake." He cringed at his words. "I didn't mean—"

Her eyes narrowed. "I may be a rookie within the Marshals, Kurt, but I was a police officer before I joined. You knew that, right?"

He didn't really recall what her previous training had been before she'd been assigned to the district. "I never questioned your qualifications," he said instead.

"Well, maybe you could've used my input when dealing with the police. Because it seems clear to me that delivering the warrant should've been left with the Sheriff's Office."

"They wouldn't have made it in time. They were right behind me and were informed of what I was doing."

She exhaled, the disapproval evident on her face, but she didn't comment. "Did you know Judge Linn was responsible for bringing Rebecca here, for this job, in the first place?" She raised her eyebrows. "I didn't think so."

It was news to him. "He should've mentioned—"

"That's right. He probably didn't because deep down the judge knew the police should've been handling the threat instead of us from day one."

"And this is where experience comes in, Delaney. We take judges' requests seriously, despite motivation."

She crossed her arms over her chest. "She's pretty, isn't she?"

He flinched. "I don't see—"

"It's relevant because you've been treating her more like a partner than a protectee."

Kurt pulled his shoulders back. "And with time, you'll find that all cases are not handled equally in the Marshals. You're used to policy and procedure being laid out for you, no matter the circumstances. We're given more space to handle things the way we deem most effective given the situation."

She inhaled. "That may be, but I requested this town as my first assignment because of you."

He took a step back, surprised. He had no idea.

She held up a finger. "You have the best fugitive capture rate in the ninth circuit, and I wanted to learn from you. I was told you liked to work alone, but I didn't think you'd shut me out of your process. Clearly protection isn't your forte, and that's okay, but stop acting like you have to do this on your own. I know the judge requested you but that doesn't mean I can't partner with you. I know police work. Keep me more in the loop and let me bridge the divide."

It took a tremendous amount of self-control to keep wisecracking and defensive comments contained. Bottom line, she was right. He'd been a poor leader.

In high school, he'd liked to think of himself as a great leader. He'd brought his baseball team to state championships all four years. They'd won the title three of those years. Looking back, all he could remember was the glory of the home runs and the strikeouts he'd thrown. No wonder his team had felt he'd let them down when he'd broken his ankle. He'd never treated them like a team. There was no leadership when he did it all on his own. In the military and even in the Marshals, he either followed orders or did everything on his own. What made him think he could ever lead a team? He wasn't cut out to get a promotion.

"You're right. I haven't kept you in the loop like I should. Your input would be valued."

Her eyes widened. "Thank you. I've got some accommodations lined up for tonight. Now what?"

"Two priorities come to mind. If Rebecca is up to it, since we're already here, let's see if she can find the numbers she needs. The key to all this must be in there. Second, we need to get the identification of the security guard that shot at her. It's possible we're only dealing with one guy, and he's probably the one who murdered the accountant."

She exhaled. "Do you have any guesses at motivation?"

"None. I'm hoping Rebecca can find that missing piece."

"Okay. I can work with the Sheriff's Office to identify him."

"That'd be great. How do you feel about interviewing the owner, Mr. Cabell, as well? He's been mysteriously absent thus far."

She beamed. "I can absolutely do that. I'll get the police on a search for our suspect." She spun off and walked toward Detective Hall and the other officers.

He exhaled. He wanted to be a leader.

Rebecca was watching him. His heart surged again. Delaney was wrong about one thing. He wasn't treating Rebecca like a partner. But he wanted to, the kind of partner that he could pull into his arms after a hard day's work. He frowned and blinked the thought away.

He crossed the distance and nodded at Detective Hall before addressing the man sitting on the floor. "Mr. Putnam, did you hire the head of security?"

"No, no, no." Putnam shook his head and looked as if he was about to get woozy again. The paramedic grabbed his wrist. "Mr. Cabell hired him."

"Is it policy for your security guards to carry weapons?"

"Absolutely not. Well, except for Giomar. He has a gun, but that's because whenever Mr. Cabell travels, he goes as his personal guard." Putnam's balance wavered. "Was...was that the gunshot I heard?"

"I think we better take a little trip to the hospital," the paramedic said. "Your heart rate is erratic."

If Putnam left for the hospital, Kurt would have to

wait hours before getting the answers he needed. "Mr. Cabell needs a personal guard?" Kurt pressed.

The paramedic waved over the second guy to join him.

"I always thought he was paranoid, but he's an extremely rich man." Mr. Putnam shook his head. "It didn't seem outlandish."

The secretary, who was still quite peeved with him, rushed in front of Kurt and grabbed Mr. Putnam's briefcase. "I'll go with you to the hospital."

Rebecca gestured in the direction he'd been talking with Delaney. "I guess you heard about my grandpa's part in this."

"I'm not convinced the judge has any part, other than not wanting to sway you toward giving this place a green light with your audit."

She seemed to stand taller. "You think? That would make so much sense. He wanted to make sure I stayed impartial." She exhaled and put a hand on his arm. "Thank you."

"He should've told me, though. I imagine he wanted to make sure I didn't have any inkling to pass it on to the local P.D."

"That would be Grandpa. He'd want only the best." Her eyes glistened as she smiled at him. "I'm glad he got the best. Thank you for saving my life…again. If I'm being honest with myself, I'm starting to rethink my live-in-the-moment lifestyle."

"I'm not going to say I disagree with you, but it's not all bad. It probably means you can compartmentalize, which is what I'm hoping. I need you to forget that someone is after you for a few moments and focus on the numbers."

She sucked in a sharp breath. "It's time to get to work. Let's go find a murderer."

NINE

Rebecca's stomach growled for the fifth time in ten minutes.

Delaney looked up from her device. "I promise we don't usually starve our protectees. As soon as Kurt gets here, I'll go pick up some food."

She'd at least had a good breakfast, but that was the only thing she'd eaten all day. It seemed to be becoming a pattern. Delaney rummaged in her duffel bag and pulled out a protein bar. "Will this help?"

Her stomach growled yet again. "Apparently my stomach doesn't trust me to answer correctly. Yes, please." She ripped open the wrapper and chomped down on the nutty goodness and was pleasantly surprised at the taste of chocolate. She bit another three-inch bite and leaned back into the hotel sofa. Her laptop whirred to life on the coffee table in front of her.

Delaney had gone a different direction than the last hole-in-the-wall motel. They were now in a suite at Vista's main competitor, a resort and spa that sat right on the lake and even boasted having the world's only floating golf hole. Rebecca had yet to use any of her vacation time that'd been building for the past few years, aside from a stray day here and there to stay with her parents during the holidays. With all the traveling she did, she never craved more time in a hotel, but this resort and spa was something else.

The clock that hung on the beige wall said it was nine o'clock already. It'd taken ages for the police to have all their questions answered and to get their computer expert on the phone to help her access Levi's computer. Detective Hall had grown quite grumpy. Apparently he should've been at his daughter's concert, and he wasn't too thrilled that Kurt had enlisted Rebecca as his asset to check the files.

They'd copied all the financial files to the police's evidence cloud as well as hers. Kurt promised to make sure all evidence was deleted from it once Rebecca was done evaluating the numbers. It didn't matter that she'd pointed out that, under her auditing contract signed by Vista Resorts, she was supposed to have all of the financial files anyway.

And while she couldn't wait to dive into the numbers to understand what Levi had found, the adrenaline had dissipated. She was exhausted and hungry and frustrated that her body didn't understand that a man was out to kill her so she didn't have time to be human.

Kurt was getting a change of clothes at his place, which she didn't begrudge him since he still had brown paint on his back, but she was about to demand room service if he didn't show up soon. At least Delaney had supplied her with a couple of clean outfits. Most of the pants had elastic waists since Delaney didn't know what size she wore. They were at least comfortable.

Delaney followed her gaze. "Now that I know we're

the same size, I'll bring you some jeans in the morning."

Her phone rang. "It's the judge. Can I answer?"

Delaney nodded. "Go ahead and take it. Feel free to use one of the bedrooms for privacy."

She tried to flash a grateful smile, but as tired as she was, it might've looked more like a grimace, especially since she was trying to get herself out of the deep couch. She hit the accept button as she walked around the coffee table. "Grandpa?"

"It's so good to hear your voice, sweetie. I'm on my way back to town."

He had nothing to come back to since the bomb. An invisible heavy weight settled on her chest. She hadn't spoken to anyone in her family since the last two near misses, and the longing to be with them almost crushed her. "You know everything that happened?"

His sigh held so much weariness. "I do. I've been told I can still live in the house, though. They've got the windows all boarded up, and I've got crews coming to repair everything in the morning."

"Prepare yourself. It may be okay for you to stay there but it's going to stink. I didn't get a look after the fire was put out, but I've heard the kitchen is totally gutted."

"Don't you worry about me. I hated having such a huge house to myself, anyway. I suppose I'll be glad tonight because my room is the farthest from the dining area. Your grandma loved that kitchen." His voice wavered. "She designed it."

"I know," she whispered.

"Deputy Marshal Brock got in touch with me a few

minutes ago. Honey, I never would've recommended you for the audit if I thought I was putting you in danger. Not even for a second. I was going to tell you after you finished your report. There was no intent to deceive, though I must admit, I probably wouldn't have given Putnam's suggestion to invest a second thought if…" He coughed. "Who am I kidding? There might've been some hidden motive to get you to visit me."

Her heart twisted. So much work to get a visit from her. "I'll come more often. And you can come to Ohio anytime, you know. I don't think I'll be traveling as much." Once she got home, she would see about transferring to a position that allowed her to stay put and make connections easier.

"Let's just focus on keeping you safe for the time being. You should know I've called your father."

She gulped. "Are you two—?"

"We're still talking, for now. He's furious with me and worried about you, but since it looks like this has nothing to do with my job, I think in the end we'll be okay. I wanted to apologize for my part in this, for bringing you here. I asked your dad to let you rest so he won't call you just yet, but he's eager to speak to you. That marshal still not handsome enough to tempt you?"

She laughed at the sudden change in conversation. "Well, he is pretty handsome, Grandpa."

"That's what worries me. Is he behaving himself?"

"Of course. As if you even need to ask."

"Are you?"

She gasped at his question. A knock sounded at the hallway door. "Good night, Grandpa," she said in response. He chuckled and returned her goodbye.

She rushed out to find Kurt in the living area wearing clean jeans and a navy polo so crisp it looked ironed. He dropped a duffel bag to the ground but, sadly, nothing else was in his hands. Her shoulders drooped. "I thought you had food."

Delaney grabbed up some keys and shook her head. "Trust me, you don't want him to pick out dinner, or you'll be eating corn dogs."

Kurt smiled. "They're fifty cents at the gas station."

Her stomach would take corn dogs right now. It would take anything. "I don't care." Her appetite wasn't the problem. Given the grave situation, she had zero cravings.

Delaney hopped up. "I'll be right back with some real food. Salads okay?"

Rebecca paused for a second. "Salad is great as long as there are big hunks of meat and sticks of potatoes to go with it."

Delaney shook her head, as if disappointed Rebecca didn't have more refined or healthy tastes. "Burger and fries. Got it." The door clicked behind her as she left.

Alone again with Kurt, her energy returned. Hopefully he had a plan for what they did next. "I hear you talked to my grandpa. Any other news?"

Kurt shook his head. "The head of security hasn't been identified yet, and the owner is nowhere to be found, if that's what you're asking. The guard was using a fake name at the offices, but the police picked up his fingerprints from his desk and a coffee mug. If he has any priors or, judging by his accent, went through immigration in recent years, he'll likely be in the system." His kind eyes searched hers. "At least we can hope. How are you holding up?"

"I'm fine." Her mind was occupied on the way he'd said *hope*. "Do *you* have faith?" After their previous conversations, the question tumbled out before she could hold it back.

"In myself?"

Oh, yeah. She'd once told him she had faith in him. "No, that's not what I meant. You wouldn't be so good at your job if you didn't. I'm asking…" Her bravado failed her. Faith was a very personal topic for a lot of people. "You don't have to answer if you don't want to."

He quirked an eyebrow and smiled. "I see why you're good at auditing. You have no problem asking questions."

"I follow a thought trail, I suppose. Sometimes it's random, but it often leads me somewhere interesting."

Kurt sat on the couch and placed his cell phone and a computer next to her laptop on the coffee table. He reached into his duffel bag and pulled out a small, worn Bible. He tapped the cover. "I wouldn't feel safe without knowing someone's got my back."

She knew it. "You're a Christian."

He nodded. "Is that a problem?"

"No." She smiled. Logically she believed in God, and it comforted her that Kurt did, as well. Her belief didn't come without struggle, though. She let busyness come first before her time with God, and sometimes doubt lingered when her friends all seemed to have amazing testimonies. They'd seen evidence of God working on their behalf. But in her case, either He hadn't or she'd been too busy to notice.

Kurt tilted his head and raised an eyebrow. "Well?"

"Well, what?"

He laughed. "You get to ask me the questions, but you're not going to reciprocate?"

She placed a hand on her hip. "I didn't want to tell you things about myself if you didn't want to know. You could ask."

"I'm asking." He bent his head and swiped across the track pad on his laptop.

Kurt was truly a man of few words. She almost pointed out that he hadn't literally vocalized a question, but she obliged. "I'm a believer, but I don't have an exciting testimony. I imagine you do, given your background."

He leaned back and crossed his arms at his chest. "I suppose it depends on what you define as exciting. God loved me enough to send His son to pay the price for my sins. I'm saved and get to spend eternity with Him." He shrugged. "I think that's pretty exciting."

It was as if a hammer shattered hard parts around her heart she didn't know were there. She bit her lip and blinked back sudden tears that threatened. He was right. And she'd stayed alive all week despite a man trying to kill her. Why hadn't she taken a moment and thanked God for that? "Then I have an epic testimony."

She loved the way his grin made little lines next to his eyes. Some people called them crow's feet, but that term didn't fit at all. They were more like happy arrows to his gorgeous dark eyes. "As do I," he said. "Since junior high."

He patted the spot next to him on the couch. "I know it's late, but are you up for some detective work?"

The idea of working side by side with a handsome, intelligent man whose faith and ideals matched her own suddenly gave her the drive to answer yes and dive into the monotonous task of retracing each financial transaction. As much as she loved to live her life in the moment, wandering from one thing to the next, she still craved her parents' and grandfather's approval. That's why she'd chosen to become an accountant, albeit a traveling one. She sat and Kurt smiled. He smelled clean and fresh, as if he always smelled like pine trees and cedar.

Maybe Grandpa was right to wonder if she was behaving herself. The flippant Mr. Darcy comment she'd made earlier was now utterly untrue.

Kurt knew the police had their databases, but he also had some friends in the FBI, some military buddies who had ended up there after serving and college. It wouldn't hurt to send them a quick note to see if they could hurry the identification along. Their wheels tended to move faster than some of the state-run database retrievals.

Some time alone had done him wonders. He felt refreshed and ready to put this guy in jail before he could hurt anyone else.

Rebecca, though, probably needed food and time alone, as well. She appeared more reserved—shy, even—next to him. The laptop remained on the coffee table. She leaned over to study it but kept glancing at him as she scrolled through the rows and rows of financial information. Maybe it was too much for her to jump into work after such a long day.

He'd almost lost her today. His chest tightened at the memory. She'd been shot at and, while he'd stepped in, the fact remained that someone had pointed a gun at her. Most people didn't brush off that sort of experience and go about their regular day. "Hey," he said before really thinking about what was going to come out of his mouth next.

She set down her laptop. "What? Did you notice something?"

"You."

She blinked rapidly and her mouth opened slightly. "Oh."

"I mean I should've asked you how you were doing earlier. If you need someone to talk to—I would be glad to listen—or if you need a list of professionals…"

She tilted her head and narrowed her eyes in confusion.

Maybe she was in denial or something. He placed a friendly hand on her wrist. Only, when he touched her, heat traveled up his arm. He pulled back, cleared his throat and stared at the image of the lake framed on the wall ahead of him. "You were shot at. People usually need to talk the first time that happens."

She inhaled sharply. "Oh. That. Oh." She folded her hands in her lap. "I guess I was thinking more about everything else that's happened, been happening."

"When I arrived, Delaney said the judge was on the phone with you. You two really are close, aren't you?" It was another reminder that he could never stand a chance with Rebecca if the judge didn't approve of him.

She sighed at the same time as saying yes.

"Oh, I almost forgot." He leaned forward and pulled out a box of tea from his bag. "I stopped and picked this up on my way here. It's not food, but I noticed you seemed to like a cup before bed. Did I get the right—"

She placed a hand on her chest and leaned forward.

"That was so sweet," she whispered. Her gaze drifted to his lips and she didn't move away.

The box of tea fell from his hand. She closed her eyes and tilted her head. He reached for her—

The beep of the hotel card key sounded, followed by the click of the door handle. Rebecca flinched and jumped as far away from him as possible on the tiny love seat. His hand stayed in midair as the door swung open.

"Delivery," Delaney called out.

He moved his hand to rub his forehead. What had just happened? Had he really almost kissed her? Maybe he was the one who needed to talk to someone, because he'd obviously lost his mind.

Even if they overcame the family rule, she was going to be back to Ohio as soon as they caught the guard. There was no future for them. He needed to remember that because if she looked at him that way again...

Delaney set two brown bags of food on the table. "I hope you're still hungry because I bought a lot of value meals."

Rebecca's eyes seemed to glaze over. She shook her head. "One second. I just remembered a number when...well, I just remembered."

Kurt had read that strong surges of emotions could help people recall things. Since they'd been talking about her almost being shot, maybe she'd remembered more of what she'd seen just before she was attacked the first time.

She typed a number into the search box at the top of the screen. Several highlighted rows of numbers lined up on the screen. She pointed to the fast-food bags with one hand as her other hand clicked and swiped over the keyboard and track pad. "Could you bring me one of those?"

Delaney frowned but brought the grease-covered bag over. Kurt had never seen a woman inhale a cheeseburger so fast, and with one hand, to boot.

Her hand hovered over the keyboard. She glanced between Delaney and Kurt and shrugged. "What? You people didn't feed me, and math requires brain food."

Delaney smothered a laugh. "Fair enough."

"Come on, numbers. Tell me a story." Rebecca completely ignored them and hunched over the keys. Her eyes moved rapidly across the screen. She dropped the rest of the food on top of the wrapper as she typed and scrolled speedily for the next few minutes.

Kurt almost held his breath watching her work. She may have had a desire to work in law enforcement, and her father may have suggested accounting, but Rebecca excelled at it. And from his perspective, it was all her.

"Aha! That's where it veered." She clapped and shoved a finger at the screen. "Okay. So, I figured out where the numbers Levi had on the flash drive were hidden within the company records. If I didn't know what to look for, I would've never found it."

"What does it mean?"

She cringed. "That's the tough part. I'm not a hundred percent sure. What I do know is that Vista had bought land in the area a few years back. There's nothing outright shady about that, right? But then they took out millions of dollars in loans to build vacation homes, presumably to rent out to guests who wanted a more private vacation. They did this here and in Colorado, where their other resort is located." She took a sip of water. "If I had to guess… I think Levi discovered that the loan money was diverted into Mr. Cabell's offshore account. Technically speaking, to an auditor like me that's not enough to raise eyebrows because it is still a company account. It's common to avoid taxes. What's troubling is that the official company record shows the loan money going to the builders. That's where the discrepancy is."

Kurt had no idea what the discrepancy meant, so he stayed silent.

She opened up a national real-estate website and entered some of the property lots named in the company accounts. Kurt whistled at the gorgeous homes with vaulted windows and hot tubs and landscaping. "Those look like they would bring in a pretty penny."

"They bought the land for pennies on the dollar because they purchased it during the economic crash." Rebecca frowned. "But there's no income coming in from them yet. And it's been years." She turned to him.

"Why would that be worth killing an accountant over?" Delaney asked.

"I was hoping you would know that part." She ate a few fries. The fan on the air conditioner kicked in, as if mocking how hard they were thinking.

"Maybe there's something shady going on inside the vacation rentals? Drug trafficking or something. That would explain why there's no listed income," Rebecca suggested.

Delaney nodded. "Possible. Those locations are remote, miles outside of town, up in the hills. I could contact the county's Joint Agency Task Force and see if they have any reason for us to get a warrant to search one of them."

"Good idea," Kurt said. "Please do that."

Rebecca pointed at the listings on her screen. "Either way, it wouldn't hurt to drive by some of these properties. Given the suspicions, I'll need to take some photographs to match the assessor's report before my audit can be complete."

"Okay. We'll start in the morning and go to that property with three houses listed in a close radius. Delaney, while you're contacting the task force, could you also contact Detective Hall with our update? See if he'd like to send some men to join us."

If he'd taken the time to get to know Delaney, he would've been able to utilize her police background earlier.

He considered Rebecca's comment. "I'm glad to accommodate and help you take photos for your report, but I need to make it clear that if there is any reason for me to get out of the vehicle, you must stay inside." He didn't need another incident like today. He wouldn't give her a chance to wander.

"Understood." She didn't make eye contact. Whether it was from embarrassment at her actions earlier or the almost kiss, he didn't know. His own neck heated at the thought. At least Delaney would be staying in the hotel, as well. Not that he needed a chaperone, but he wouldn't turn one down, either.

Rebecca stood. "Until tomorrow." She left the living room and closed the bedroom door behind her. Her words still rang in his ears. There was a Bible verse in Matthew that basically said not to worry about tomorrow because tomorrow would bring its own worries.

Despite himself, he whispered a prayer that tomorrow's worries wouldn't involve any more danger for Rebecca...or his heart.

TEN

Rebecca had loved the thick rows of trees in the hills until someone had tried to kill her. Now she wondered what was lurking in the forests surrounding her favorite small town. In the side mirror, the lake, the suite that had the most comfortable bed she'd ever slept in and the floating golf green grew smaller as they drove.

Kurt's GPS narrated directions. Delaney drove a blue van behind them. The police had sent a couple of plain clothes officers to follow them, as well. This way there would be a car for each house, in case Mr. Cabell turned out to be hiding or running nefarious activities in one of them.

She'd fought so hard to finish the job set in front of her, but it hit her that her striving would all be for nothing. "Let's say I take photos of the house, tidy up my audit and send my boss the report. It would satisfy my contract, but really, it doesn't matter anymore. There's no way Grandpa will invest, and I highly doubt Mr. Putnam will be publishing my work as a third-party review to get more investors."

Kurt nodded but didn't say anything. Oh, great. He was back to being the Silent Marshal when she thought they'd finally moved past that. Why had she tried to kiss him? Okay, the reasons were sitting right in front of her, but she didn't want her lapse in judgment to cause problems between them. "I'm sorry I tried to kiss you."

He didn't even look at her but gave a short nod again.

She crossed her arms across her chest. "Are you giving me the silent treatment?"

"Of course not." The GPS notified him to take a turn. A dirt road was visible about a hundred feet in front of them. He touched the far side of his head, which she knew held an earpiece. "Ready to split up?" He paused. "Affirmative." He touched his ear again then sighed. "Rebecca, I think it might be best if we stuck to conversations about the case. Like you said, the threat is probably over once you're done with the report, and you're about to have the final piece in minutes."

That hurt. It made sense, but she wanted to still have the friendly conversation. She had vague notions they would keep in touch. Despite the danger, her time in Coeur d'Alene felt more like home than Ohio. Maybe it was because her favorite memories were summer moments with the mountains, bright blue lake and trees. She exhaled and looked out the window. Foolish daydreams. "Fair enough."

"I'll slow down in front of each of the properties. It should be enough for you to grab a photograph, but I'm not stopping until the third house. That's when you'll stay in the vehicle."

"Why the third?" She knew he didn't want to talk

much, but she couldn't hold back her curiosity. Besides, this was technically about the case.

"Our map may be outdated, but I know that the third property is a dead end surrounded by high cliffs. The only way in is the dirt road." He took a sharp turn. "Here we go."

"You want two cars between me and a potential threat following us."

He nodded. "You catch on fast."

"Your location is on the right. You have arrived," the stilted voice announced from his phone.

So the first house should be on the right, but the property was covered in evergreen trees. "No sign of a driveway yet." She squinted, trying to see if the house was buried deep in the trees. Luxury vacationers did appreciate ultraprivate venues, especially with clients who dealt with a bit of fame. "Maybe GPS isn't as accurate as we hoped and it's up ahead. It wouldn't have been the first time. They're not the most accurate when there aren't city roads."

Kurt slowed his speed and picked up his phone. "No, this should be right."

The dirt road curved around a few mounds of dirt. Odd. The road, in and of itself, wasn't ideal for vacationers if they had inclement weather, but the mounds of dirt should've been gone by now. In the distance she spotted the cliff he was referring to. It wouldn't take long to reach the end of the road at this rate. The tops of the mountains still had a thick layer of snow that wouldn't melt until summer. "Kurt, there's nothing here. There are no houses."

"It would appear you're right."

Yet she'd seen the images of the vacation homes

in the records from the appraiser. "Mortgage fraud." She shook her head. "I can't believe I didn't think of it before now. This is why Levi found it when no one else did. His sister was in real estate, and he was selling his own land so this type of thing would've been on his radar. Maybe he'd noticed they weren't bringing in income yet and wanted to look at the vacation houses himself."

"Well that'll at least give Detective Hall a place to start with motive for murder. Otherwise, it seems this trip out here has been a waste of time."

"Not for me. My boss will be thrilled we discovered fraud. It boosts the company's reputation, another selling tool for third-party auditors." In fact, she wouldn't be surprised if a raise or a promotion would be in her future. A month ago the thought would've excited her, but it didn't even make her smile now.

The sun glinted off something metallic. She squinted. Her eyes were either playing tricks on her, especially given how far away it was, but the Hummer might be hidden behind the trees. She leaned closer to the passenger window and put her hand on the glass to block the sun. "Ku—"

A loud pop hit the windshield. The laminate front glass popped and cracked, but never shattered around a bullet hole the size of a golf ball. She recoiled and her head hit the side of the door. "Someone just shot at us!" Behind her a chunk of the passenger seat was missing, with a few springs sticking out of it, the same spot where she'd just been sitting. A cry stuck in her throat as her chest seized.

The SUV spun.

"What's happening?" The momentum shifted her

head back into the headrest but her left shoulder had nothing to rest on, a reminder that someone wanted her heart to stop beating.

"Keep your head down!" Kurt grabbed her hand and pulled as he kept his other hand on the steering wheel. His hand moved from her wrist to her back, as if to make her stay down. He didn't need to tell her twice. His hand left and she felt movement behind her into the back seat, where he kept his weapons. The vehicle jolted to a stop. "Stay put!"

She turned her head to the side, her cheek practically touching her knee. Kurt had a rifle in his hand. He rolled out of the SUV, took a knee, aimed and fired twice. He jumped back into the vehicle, the rifle in his lap, and took off, barreling forward.

"What happened? Can I sit up?"

"Are you injured? Were you hit?" His voice was terse.

"I'm fine. Stop answering my questions with questions."

"Stay down until the threat is clear." He swerved the SUV and jumped out again. She heard footsteps and shouts but didn't hear gunshots. Her stomach cramped in the uncomfortable position. She inched her head up until she could peek past the dashboard.

Delaney had pulled the van into a diagonal position. The police car behind her had stopped in an opposite position, and another set of officers stood behind their SUV with Kurt. Their guns were down, but they all spoke into phones.

Kurt pointed toward the SUV. He was heading back to her. She ducked her head.

The door creaked open. "You can sit up now, I

think. Delaney thinks I hit the target. We have more units on the way."

"You hit the shooter? How is that possible? I never even saw him. How'd you know where he was?"

He sat down in the driver's seat. "I could tell the trajectory of where the bullet came from. It's not a windy day, and I trained as a sharpshooter." He shrugged with the last statement as if it was no big deal.

It was a huge deal to her. She opened her mouth to say so but a wet spot grew on his shoulder. "You're bleeding! Were you shot?"

"I'm sure it was from the seat or a spring or something. It's just a scratch. I'm fine."

She reached for him. "No, you're not."

He gathered her fingers before she could investigate. "Yes, I am." His grip loosened and he shook his head. "I keep thinking I'm going to lose you." He pulled her fingers ever so slightly toward his face, as if he was going to kiss her hand. After saving her life for what seemed like the millionth time, that simply wouldn't do. She reached for his neck with her other hand, leaned over the console and kissed his cheek.

Her heart pounded in her throat as he dropped her hand. His palms moved to cradle either side of her face. Their eyes met and she leaned forward until their lips touched. All her gratitude, devotion and unsaid feelings seemed to be held in that kiss. Who was she kidding? She didn't want to have a long-distance friendship with this man. She was falling head over heels.

At the sound of a throat being cleared, Kurt's hands dropped away and he broke the kiss. Rebecca dropped fully into her seat, well, what was left of it. Delaney stood in front of the still-open driver's door with her hands on her hips and a smirk on her face. The officers standing next to the SUV chuckled, openly staring, and one let out a hearty "Woot."

"If you're ready," Delaney said with slow emphasis. "And for future reference, the tinted windows don't do much good if the door is open."

"He was bleeding," Rebecca said and realized it really didn't make sense as an excuse.

Delaney's smirk evolved into a toothy grin. "If you're okay, Kurt, we've discovered a road that leads to where we believe the shooter waited. One of the officers discovered an electronic box used for an invisible trip wire. The shooter was probably alerted in plenty of time to get into position."

The air evaporated from Rebecca's lungs. Any normal fugitive would never have the resources to electronically secure a hiding spot in the woods.

"Who *is* this guy?" Kurt exclaimed. "Why don't we have his identification yet?"

"Why would he hide here? Unless it was a test," Rebecca murmured.

"Test? What are you talking about?"

"At the offices, he said he didn't want to kill me, but I wouldn't let it go. Maybe he set up the invisible trip wire more as a trap than security."

"To see if you'd let it go?" Kurt's stomach twisted.

Delaney shook her head. "The officers are about to search the Hummer." Delaney pointed at Rebecca. "Are you okay if we examine the shooting scene, or do I need to take you back to the hotel while they do?"

"I think I'm fine."

"Why don't you ride with Delaney?" Kurt's question sounded more like an order. He kept his gaze straight ahead.

It felt like a vise around her throat. They'd kissed a moment ago and he was already pushing her away. It was as if she was a human yo-yo. "Yes, that makes sense." She blinked away the burning sensation of held-back tears. "Since I don't have a fully functioning seat," she added. She knew it wasn't the real reason he suggested she get away from him, but she couldn't help but try to save face in front of Delaney.

Delaney's smile had faded. There was no fooling her, either. "Yeah, that seat isn't safe," Delaney said. "I could use the company. Some weirdo stocked the CD player with nothing but classical music."

He was pretty sure *Do not kiss your protectee, especially in front of other law-enforcement peers* was probably an unwritten rule in the Marshals service. Kurt followed the blue van through the forested area near the Hummer. Behind, and to the right of the vehicle, was a hidden dirt path that wound up a hill to the cliff area. While it was not wide enough to be a standard road, he felt sure they could make it.

Delaney drove painstakingly slow, no doubt keeping a sharp eye out for more trip wires. Kurt hated that he hadn't been observant enough to spot one on the way in. His failure had put Rebecca in harm's way yet again.

He'd caught the look of hurt on Rebecca's face when she'd left the SUV to ride with Delaney. That kiss had made everything so much more difficult. He tried so hard not to wear his heart on his sleeve, but he rarely succeeded. It was part of the reason he worked alone so much of the time. Self-preservation. Which is why he needed Rebecca as far away as possible while close enough that he could still protect her. He was losing his heart, and fast, and if he didn't reel it back in, she'd take it with her across the country.

The SUV hopped around the uneven terrain as he followed behind the van until they reached the top of the cliff. Delaney exited the van first, her hand on her weapon. She pointed to the tire tracks heading in the opposite direction down the hill. "Tread makes me think it's a small ATV. Better call it in and get the police on it."

He walked the ledge until he found the perfect spot to view the entire road below. Right beside his foot was a patch of blood. A couple of feet beyond it, the shell of a hollow point, the bullet of choice to go through a windshield, rested in a groove of dirt.

"You hit him." Delaney looked over her shoulder, the phone still on her ear. "Yeah, we're going to need a kit. We've got a blood sample."

The amount of blood suggested a scratch more than a direct hit. It appeared he'd barely nicked the man. So much for his sharp-shooting days. He didn't hold on to hope that it had slowed the man down, but at least it had scared him enough to move on after one bullet. "Let the police take the lead on this. Let's get Rebecca back to town. Is the judge back?"

Delaney hung up and nodded. "Deputy Marshal Eric Ashton just delivered him to his house. He's personally overseeing the construction crew. He says windows go back in today before they work on the interior. He'll also install the alarm and surveillance system."

"Good, but I don't think the judge can stay there.

This guy has surprised us at every turn. He beat the system we set up before. I wouldn't put it past our suspect to kidnap the judge as a way to get to Rebecca."

"This whole thing seems pretty extreme to cover up mortgage fraud."

He agreed. While the fraud did constitute millions, the lengths the supposed security guard went to just to silence Rebecca surprised him, as well. Was it possible there was more they'd yet to uncover?

"Let's go back and coordinate with Ashton to make a new plan."

She nodded and went back to the van.

Rebecca stared out the window as if neither of them existed. And while he wanted to talk to her privately, to help her understand where he was coming from, it would do no good. She would still be leaving soon, and it might be easier on both of them, if she stayed mad. He hopped into the SUV, found the classical radio station and let Chopin accompany him all the way back to the resort.

Delaney and Rebecca had already made it to the hotel hallway when he joined them. Delaney reached for the doorknob. "Hold up," he called. He'd forgotten to let Delaney know he'd placed a marker in the hinges. He was trying to be a better leader, but letting other people into his thought process wasn't second nature yet.

"I placed a—" He exhaled. The small piece of blue paper he'd stuck in between the door and the frame on the hinge side was on the floor. The paper was the same shade as the carpet, so in the event the door was opened an intruder wouldn't notice it on the ground when he left. The do-not-disturb sign still hung on the door, so it was unlikely to be housekeeping.

"Get out." He took Rebecca's hand. She squeezed his hand and ran with him toward the exit of the building. Kurt pulled his weapon and scanned the outdoors.

Delaney had her weapon out, scanning behind them. "What's going on?"

"I need you to evacuate the building. I'm taking Rebecca to the off-site location. Tell Deputy Ashton to get the judge and meet us there."

Her eyes widened. "What?"

"Someone's been in the room. I placed a marker as a precaution after the bomb at Justice Linn's place. I think we need to utilize our off-site location."

"Kurt, are you sure—"

"Clear this wing of the hotel and call SWAT and ATF to check the room." He knew Delaney wanted him to give up protection of Rebecca to the police. Rebecca seemed to take a step closer to his arm, as if she was also aware of what Delaney was about to say.

Delaney resigned herself to a nod. "I'll guard you until you get back in the vehicle."

"Call me the moment they find out what's in the room." He swallowed hard. "I hope I'm overreacting." If not, everyone in the resort was in danger.

"You and me both," Delaney answered as she ran toward the resort office to start the evacuation process.

He let go of Rebecca's hand. "Stay close behind me." She placed a hand on his back, which helped him focus, knowing exactly where she was. He kept his weapon down low until he put Rebecca in the back seat of the SUV. He scanned the roofline and any other venues around him that could be used by a sniper. Nothing. He hopped into the driver's side.

"I know it's an awkward situation, but do I really have to sit in the back seat?"

Kurt almost groaned. The woman seemed to thrive on conflict, more specifically resolving conflict. Couldn't they just leave things unsaid and let them fester like normal people? "The windshield has been compromised once. It's safer for you to be in the back, especially if someone is watching."

"Oh. Was that the reason you had me ride with Delaney, as well?"

He saw the hope in her eyes from the rearview mirror. His gut twisted, but he couldn't deal with it at the moment. "Can we discuss that later? I need to focus on getting to the boat launch. We can't have anyone follow us."

"That's what's been bothering me. There's no way that guy could've beat us from the cliff to the resort and set up a bomb in time."

"True. And you're probably right. I probably overreacted, but after the pipe bomb slipped past our noses and the trip wire…"

"You don't want to take any chances with our lives. It was the right call."

He didn't want to mention the story he vividly remembered from his training days. A man in WITSEC had stepped out of the program. The guy had returned home and turned his doorknob. The bomb had made sure he never took another breath.

Kurt hadn't realized how on edge he'd been since the pipe bomb incident until now. He had knots in his neck. He prayed he was wrong and nothing came of the hotel marker being moved, but mostly he prayed that the Lord would help them keep everyone safe.

He pulled into the shared marina that all local law enforcement used. It had the most security. "Come on."

"I didn't know the Marshals had a boat here."

He laughed. "That's the point." The sheriff boat had big lettering on all sides, but the Marshals preferred to stay under the radar. The philosophy was true about everything they did. They were most effective without the whole world knowing how they worked.

On any other day, he would've relished the chance to take the boat out for a spin. Lake Coeur d'Alene was twenty-five miles long, three miles wide at one point and had over one hundred miles of shoreline. There was so much potential for someone trying to hide, which was why the Marshals owned a boat.

After a seven-mile drive on the water, far from prying eyes, they would reach a near-invisible boat dock. Nestled on one of the many eastern foothills, it was far from any highway, advantageous for safety. They used it only in the most extreme case, as it was difficult to access and devoid of cell signal. The last time they'd used it was two years ago for a witness about to testify.

Their soles tapped in rhythm on the wooden pier. The waves slapped against the hull of the boat. A bald eagle cried out as it dove for unseen food. The area served as a migratory spot for the eagles, so it wasn't an uncommon sight, yet it still took his breath away every time he saw the majestic creatures.

The breeze carried Rebecca's curls away from her face. "I love this place. I love the sounds, the sights… I hate that we're running away from something instead of to something."

He stepped over the edge of the boat and took her hand to help her. He steeled himself just in time for the reaction his heart made at her touch. "I'm not sure what you mean."

She stepped fully on board and faced him. "I'm saying you were right. We need to be sensitive to what the Lord has for us, but it's time to make a plan."

The way she talked as if they were a couple took him off guard.

His phone vibrated, but he needed her safe before he answered. He hurried her to the center of the aluminum boat. Like most of their law-enforcement boats, it had a fully sealed cabin where he could drive safely without being in the open. He unlocked the trunk that doubled as seating and pulled out two ballistic vests and two life jackets. "It's not the most comfortable thing, but I need you to wear both. Ballistic on first."

He pulled out his phone. His contact at the FBI had texted him.

We've identified your guy. You've got yourself a big problem.

ELEVEN

There was very little room to move in the tin box with windows. She bumped into Kurt twice trying to maneuver to the seat next to the radio controls.

"I need your phone."

She handed it to him without question. He placed the phone in a thick, zippered bag similar to the one he'd used when he'd first showed up in her life. Even though she wasn't supposed to use her phone unless there was an emergency, it had been a small comfort to have it. Without her computer, she had no way of communicating with the outside world. "I thought your IT guy already made sure there was no spyware."

"He did, but the situation has changed. We need to take extra precautions." He cranked the engine and drove like a madman on the choppy waters.

"You seem more upset than usual." She had to almost yell. There was not one, but three motors on the back of the boat. If it had been summer and there wasn't someone intent on taking her life, it might've actually been fun. The way Kurt's jaw muscles were working stressed her out. He had new information, she was sure of it. "What is it?"

"We now know the identity of the security guard that's been trying to kill you."

"Oh?" His tone suggested the man's identity had significance. "Is it a name I would recognize?"

He gave her a sidelong glance, as if trying to decide whether to share the information or not.

"Information is power," she said by way of encouragement.

He smirked. "One you have to use responsibly." He sighed. "He used to work for a private military in a different country."

"Used to?" They passed some floating houses that were occupied only in the summer months.

"My source says he was equivalent to our Special Forces. The US, on occasion, contracts the private guys, but, according to my friend, the pay is minimal. They're hungry and not picky about the work, so when we're done using them…"

"Mr. Cabell snapped him up?"

"It appears so. That's not the problem." He turned a sharp corner as the wind whipped up some impressive waves. The lake narrowed as they left the tourist zone, as she liked to call it. Inlets covered in evergreen trees jutted into the water until it resembled a winding river.

"I'm a little afraid to ask."

"You should be. I can deal with one former contract soldier. Now that we know who we're working with, we can outnumber him and beat him at his own techniques. But the FBI got an alert that a group of mercenaries entered the country. They used to work for the same private military. The Bureau had to make sure they weren't on FBI assignment before letting me know."

"You're not saying they're coming here, are you?"

"I'm saying it's likely they *are* here, as of today, or they're arriving right now."

The hull crashed through another wave. Her stomach dropped, more from the news than gravity. "They want me dead that badly?"

He frowned but didn't reply, which was answer enough. His phone buzzed and he lowered the throttle. He lifted the phone to read it, but she managed to catch a glimpse, as well.

Tried to call. You must be out of range. Hope this comes through. Bomb disarmed. Attached to light switch. Everyone safe.

It had to be from Delaney. "The light switch had the bomb?"

"The light switch would've been the trigger. I've seen it before, often in meth labs." He hung his head and exhaled before pressing the throttle back to full speed. "I had hoped I was wrong."

"That's why the guard—the private military guy— was able to try to shoot us and set the bomb so fast. He assigned someone else to the bomb. How'd they know where we were?"

"If they have the training and technology that the FBI described, it wouldn't have mattered that we cleared your phone of spyware. We need to be thankful the mercenaries just arrived, or we likely would've been ambushed last night. Let's get you to safety so I can make that plan. I'm going to demand reinforcements. It might be tricky since officially these military guys don't exist. For now, I'm going to need you to help keep watch."

The next ten minutes passed in tense silence, not counting the buzz of the motors and the slaps the boat made when hitting waves. It seemed surreal. The speed decreased and Kurt made a sudden turn. She lost her balance and fell backward. His arms wrapped around her. The motors died. He cradled her head in his elbow while his other hand caught her lower back. He'd kept her head from hitting the controls.

"Thank you."

His eyes softened. "It was my fault. I almost missed our turn."

She lifted her chin to see his face and, for a moment, it almost appeared as if he considered kissing her.

He pulled her up to standing, a small smile on his face. "You're not making it easy on me, are you?"

She blinked, replaying his words in her head. "You mean keeping me safe?"

He shook his head. "No, that's not what I mean." The motor hummed back to life as he gently pressed the throttle. The small inlet opened up when he turned the second corner to reveal a pier, hidden from sight from the main waters. "Welcome to Ambush Alcove." He raised the trunk lid and grabbed some weapons stashed there. "We have a little hike."

"Why do they call it Ambush?"

"Because hopefully that's what we'll be able to do if anyone comes near here. It's situated like a fortress because once we get to the cabin we can see everything for miles. We can see someone approaching from every direction and we can—"

"Got it." She helped tie off one side of the boat to the dock before she removed the vests and stepped out. Her legs wobbled for a moment, as if still on the water.

She followed Kurt uphill across rocky terrain. They passed a few boulders and trees until they reached a set of wooden stairs. Her legs objected to the steep incline. She needed food. Her stomach grumbled at the thought. "Another reason I'm thankful I didn't end up in law enforcement. I like food too much." Her words came out on heavy breaths as she chugged after him.

He laughed. "What makes you think I don't like food?"

"Ever since I've met you, I've eaten half as much as usual."

"I admit it can be feast and famine when I'm searching for fugitives." He peeked over his shoulder at her. "We don't usually starve our protectees." He refocused his gaze above. "Not too much farther."

They reached a platform. To the right, two metal poles ran horizontally down a steep incline but disappeared into a thick patch of bushes. "It has a rail system to the dock?"

He laughed. "Not one we've used since I've been here. I think it's one of the relics, like the one your grandparents had. It's pretty well hidden."

He pointed to the left. "We're going the old-fashioned way." Ropes suspended a wooden bridge.

"You've got to be kidding me." She stood on tiptoe and peered over the edge. It wasn't that big of a drop. They could probably climb down then climb back up, but the tree branches would get in the way. "A lot of those relic systems still work. It's safe and slow, like a stair lift or really slow tram. I could wait here while you run it down."

"I'm not sure it's currently connected to the generator." He held out his hand. "You have nothing to fear."

She scoffed. "Except foreign, rogue Special Forces who've likely been contracted to kill me."

His eyes searched hers for a long moment. "When I was deployed, and probably more so when I track down a fugitive, I make it a point to remember that if I give in to fear, my ability to act logically and rationally diminishes…sometimes disappears."

She related. It's why she stayed busy, lived in the moment, didn't take time to stop to analyze her feelings. Her heart pounded against her chest. Had she realized the reasons why before?

Kurt must have taken her silence for agreement. He squeezed her hand. "I can find dozens of verses that tell me not to fear and not to be afraid. I also found dozens of verses that told me to fear the Lord." He tilted his head and smiled. "But because we both know Him, we know He loves us and is for us, not against us." He shrugged. "I don't know if that does anything for you, but I feel peace every time I remember."

"It's not an excuse to be foolish," she shot back. Her chest tightened. She wanted to take the time to really think about his words, but all she could see was the bridge waving ever so slightly in the breeze.

He laughed. "No, you're right. In my opinion, it would be foolish to try to go the distance on foot. And, personally, if we could survive the fall into the Spokane River then this will be a piece of cake. You once said you had faith in me, too. Did you mean it?"

She groaned. "I should know by now to keep my

thoughts to myself around people with good memories." She held out her hand for him to take. "Make it fast." The first step onto the bridge was the hardest as it had the biggest dip. Her other hand reached the knotted rope and slid because Kurt was true to his word. He raced across the bridge. His gentle tugging pulled her so fast the passage hardly had a chance to sway.

Her feet touched solid ground and he beamed. "How's that for living in the moment?" He dropped her hand and waved her to a final set of steps.

"I told you. I'm ready to turn over a new leaf. Pray and plan." Halfway up the last flight the cabin came into focus. It wasn't much, but the wood paneling and the green roof did do a nice job of camouflage. She just hoped her prayers were working fast enough to give Kurt a good plan.

Kurt typed in the code to unlock the door. He stepped inside and covered his mouth. The smell of cedar and pine were stronger inside the cabin than outside. A coiled rug was rolled up and propped up against the side of the wall, so the floor had nothing on it but a thick layer of dust, some that he'd stirred up by coming inside.

Rebecca coughed behind him. "I don't suppose anyone comes to clean up here."

"That's not exactly a priority in our budget." He pointed to a cupboard. "But we do keep food and water up here at all times."

She opened the door and held up a few packets. "Cheesy Alfredo rice…hearty potato soup." She flipped over the package. "Add boiling water." She spun around in a circle. "Is there a kitchen to boil water?"

"Um, I didn't promise the food would taste any good."

"You've kept witnesses here before?"

"Usually only short-term, right before and during a trial. I haven't personally escorted any big names here, but I've heard that back in the seventies...well, I can't say."

"Instant coffee. No cream or sugar. You're going to be hurting," she said.

So she'd noticed how he took his coffee. He was used to drinking caffeine without fixings, but it didn't mean he liked it. The windows were strategically placed, so he could get a full-circle view. Aside from an empty countertop, a lone futon and metal cabinets between each window, the room was empty. He unlocked a second cabinet and pulled out the satellite phone, laptop and binoculars.

The binoculars had been in a case, so he didn't need any cleaner before he raised them to his eyes. The lake reflected the deep blue sky. A gorgeous view, but the water remained still, which meant there were no boats heading their way. "I'll ask Delaney to bring you something, but I need to let her know there's been a change in plan. We can't have anyone else come in the sheriff boat."

"Why not?"

"As soon as the mercenaries realize that they didn't hit their mark, they'll be looking for you. I imagine they already have eyes on your grandpa. A sheriff boat escort down the lake is going to be on their radar." He kicked the dusty black futon and let the air particles settle before he took a seat. "It'll take Delaney a bit to wrap up with ATF and SWAT. First, I need to get Mr. Cabell's photo to my FBI guy. My sources have found squat on his location."

The laptop, unlike most of the things in the cabin, was relatively up-to-date. It was a special fields-op operating system that didn't require constant updating. A good thing, or he'd be sitting for hours before getting any work done. It whirred to life and connected to a secure satellite so he could search all the usual websites he used when hunting a fugitive. Cabell wasn't active on any social networks from what he could tell, so getting a more updated photo didn't look likely. The only hit they had was the photo accessible through the driver's license database.

Rebecca blew off dust from two water bottles and crossed the room to offer him one. She looked down at the screen. "Who's that?"

"I thought you would've known. It's the owner of Vista Resorts, Mr. Cabell."

Her eyebrows rose. "I don't know who that is, but it's definitely not Mr. Cabell."

"What do you mean? Are you sure? Look closer. It's an old photo. Not the best resolution."

She pursed her lips and squinted. "Photos don't change the physical shape of someone's entire head and face." She leaned back and held a finger in the air. "Nope, that man is not the owner of Vista Resorts. I've seen the guy and while I was never personally introduced, Mr. Howard pointed him out when we were discussing souvenirs my first day there. And then I spotted him the second day when I was…well, anyway I saw him, and he didn't look happy."

"I've looked on the website and everyone has looked for brochures around the corporate offices. Detective Hall doesn't have a single photo, either, except this license."

She rolled her eyes. "Then he's using a fake identity. I can prove it, but you have to promise not to laugh."

That sounded promising. "Where is your proof?"

"On my phone."

"Of course it is." He crossed the room and picked up the black bag he'd put her phone inside. "This thing is essentially a Faraday cage in a bag so it blocks all electromagnetic signals so no one can track us while we use it. We're supposed to be able to use the device within the container, but I've never had a need to access anything in it before. Let's hope it works."

He unzipped the first layer of fabric and pulled it down, revealing an opaque sheet that allowed him to see the screen and operate the phone, though the images weren't as clear as he'd hoped they would be. She'd followed him to the counter, so he handed her the bag. "It won't always respond to first touch, so press hard and keep at it."

She set the unit on the counter so he could look over her shoulder. She pressed the icon for photographs and frowned. "They're not here. None of my photographs are here. Would your IT guy have deleted them?"

"Of course not. If he had a reason to do so, I would've been notified." Thumbnail images of landscape photos appeared in the other album boxes. "Are you sure they're not hiding in the rest of your photographs?"

She shook her head and tapped over to the list of

albums. "Look. The entire selfie category has been deleted." She tapped on the deleted photos album and found the section empty. "I'm telling you I had tons of photos that are suddenly gone." She turned to him and paled. "The guy…the security guard…" She set the bag down and paced back and forth over the wooden floor. "That night the guard tried to take me… We've already proved he switched the flash drive, but I never thought he'd have messed with my phone. If he was able to override the security system, my phone must've been like child's play. So, maybe he knew I took a photo of his boss and deleted it."

Any detail of her hypothesis could be wrong, but the trajectory and motivation made sense. "But it became apparent to the guard that you were going to make sure you uncovered the fraud…and his boss. You're the only one that was witness to the information on the flash drive."

"Yes, but only for a second. Even though I knew enough to check those properties, I can't recreate what was on the drive. It's possible Levi had discovered more fraud that they've covered up by now. They don't know I'm clueless, though."

"Maybe we can have some employees do a sketch of him, but that's going to take time. Apparently he never let anyone take his picture."

She pointed to his computer "Maybe the photo is on my cloud account? Levi's cloud didn't have the information we wanted, but it had enough to get a warrant. Maybe we'll have success and find something. I did have my photos set to automatically back up there, but it only syncs with Wi-Fi. I'm not sure it would've saved a copy or not."

"We won't know until we try. Laptop it is." He sat back down on the futon and patted the space next to him.

She sat but hesitated to take the laptop from him. "Maybe you could look away while I hunt?"

"Why? Are you worried I'll see your password?"

"No, that's the last thing I care about." She groaned. "Never mind." She typed rapidly and rows after rows of thumbnails appeared on the screen. Most of the photos featured Rebecca flashing a silly expression at the camera.

He chuckled. "Those are quite the self-portraits."

"My niece, Mandy, likes it when I send her photos of the places I visit. I try to make her laugh." Rebecca had her tongue out in front of the Smithsonian. The next one, she had her arms wide in front of the Lincoln Memorial.

"You had more fun in DC than I did."

She scrolled faster through the photos. "Looks can be deceiving. It was lonely. It would've been fun to travel with someone." She didn't look at him, but her cheeks reddened. She zipped past similar photos until she reached one in front of the Vista Resorts corporate offices. In the image, she stood next to the trees and benches, her lips sticking out and her eyes crossed.

Rebecca put a hand over her image on the monitor. "That part is irrelevant." She circled her finger around the other half of the screen. She moved her finger and turned the laptop toward Kurt so he could see the man exiting the glass doors behind her. "This was taken the second day I was there, and it was the last time I saw Mr. Cabell."

Kurt frowned. The guy looked familiar, but he'd

looked over so many mug shots the past week with Rebecca that it was possible they were all blending together in his mind. He reached over and took control of the touch pad to zoom until the guy's face came more into focus. "He saw you take a photo. You can tell he's unhappy with you. I wish you had used better resolution."

She clicked her tongue. "Pardon me for not knowing you would need it."

He ignored the sarcasm because he couldn't rid himself of that nagging tingle in the back of his neck. "He looks so familiar." He copied the photograph, despite Rebecca's halfhearted objections to edit her out of the picture first, and attached it to an email to send to his buddy, Agent Jorgenson.

Not even a minute went by before the email dinged back.

Edward Mijovic. Top Ten Most Wanted list. Where'd you get this picture? Where are you?

"That's why the man looked familiar." He grinned. It wasn't his imagination.

Rebecca had both hands on either side of her face. "Why are you acting like this is good news? This is awful!"

"It's good because he's a fugitive, which means I'm about to get a whole lot of offers to help." Instead of the standard answer of being short on manpower, he'd have a joint task force coming his way before blinking an eye, which would not only guarantee Rebecca's safety, it would give him a chance to truly lead a team.

"But he's on the top ten list of wanted criminals? What'd he do?"

"Nothing as bad as you're probably imagining. He's dangerous, but not a serial killer. My buddy works in white-collar crime, so it's their Most Wanted list." He hoped that eased her mind about the type of criminal they were dealing with, though the guy had hired private military for a hit job. He had no doubt that help was on the way. "Edward Mijovic has many different aliases. His most recent involved investments in lithium mining."

She whistled. "That is a booming industry right now."

"Right now Nevada is the only legitimate operation in the States. Edward claimed he found a lithium mine in South Dakota, a sure moneymaker if you were one of the first investors. When the victims wanted to see the mine for themselves, Mijovic showed them an impressive location with all the right machinery. The FBI discovered he'd merely rented the equipment for a day and set it up at an abandoned mine. He didn't even own the land himself, but he had impressive websites and forgeries. He bilked investors out of millions."

He tapped the laptop and pointed at the man's picture. "The way he works is like an elaborate Ponzi scheme. He always appoints a CEO to be the face of the company."

"Like Mr. Putnam is for Vista Resorts."

"Exactly. As long as his photo isn't anywhere, he's not easy to track. He's bold enough to move from state to state, always with a new identity, and set up shop." He avoided mentioning the open murder cases associated with each scheme. No doubt, Mijovic had contracted mercenaries to do his dirty work there, as well. "He probably used some of the millions from previous cons to open the resort."

"Do you think Putnam knew? Grandpa said it was his idea to invest. Putnam wasn't pressuring him, but what if he's just an excellent con man?"

"I don't know. If I had to guess, I imagine Putnam and all of the employees thought they were working for a reputable business, but we'll be investigating to be sure."

"Part of it is a good business."

"Yes, but if history is repeating itself, Cabell's getting investors while committing mortgage fraud on the side. He's slipped through the FBI's fingers countless times."

"He's good at it. I would've missed it, if not for Levi." She blinked rapidly. "He won't slip away this time. Not with you leading the charge."

"Rebecca, I am determined to keep you safe—" His satellite phone rang. Maybe it was for the best. He'd been about to make an impulsive decision and ask her if she would ever consider staying in Ohio. Ironic. She loved that he planned, and he loved her spontaneous nature. He pushed the thought aside and answered.

Jorgenson was on the phone. Delaney had patched him through. He had a lot of coordinating to do. It was time to prepare for battle.

TWELVE

Rebecca used the binoculars the way Kurt had taught her to sweep the area from behind the safety of the windows. It afforded her a close-up view of an osprey spreading its magnificent wings to almost six feet as it dove until its beak touched the water and then swooped back up into the sky. The bird was likely catching fish, but she tried to block that thought out of her mind since she was still starving. Seafood sounded good. She'd even settle for sushi, not a favorite.

Kurt paced across the floor as he spoke on the satellite phone. It'd been his pattern for over an hour as he'd talked to numerous agencies. From the bits and pieces she'd overheard, FBI, SWAT and deputy marshals from Spokane were en route to meet Delaney at the sheriff boat.

Everything had changed since finding out Cabell was on the top ten list. Whereas Kurt didn't want anyone to notice or to follow the police boat before, now he wanted it to be easy for her attacker and his mercenaries to follow. The task force had decided to draw the mercenaries to the cove, away from the population.

If they expected gunfire and a fight to get these guys, then she wondered how they expected to keep her safe.

Kurt hung up the phone and faced her. "Your grandfather insists on coming here to be with you." He shook his head. "I'm going to make sure the rail system still works before he gets here. We should have a visual of each other the whole time. Knock on the window, hard, if you see anything."

He had her grandfather's comfort in mind—there would've been no way to get the judge up all those stairs and across the bridge—so Kurt had to have her safety in mind, as well. The only fear she should have was the fear of the Lord, and He loved her and was on her side. She exhaled and let it sink in again.

She'd never thought of herself as a fearful person, but she'd never been in danger like the past week. Her father had to take precautions, but even he had never looked a gunman in the eye. She shivered, remembering the guard's cold eyes. Pain zipped across her head like a warning sign of an impending headache, a true indication of her exhaustion. She was too tired to think anymore.

She stepped to the far edge of the window so she could watch Kurt climb down the steep hill. He grabbed hold of branches from nearby trees to stay steady and removed a knife from a pocket on the back of his belt that she hadn't noticed before. He sliced down the branches from the bush that blocked the bench seating for the rail system. He did it with such flourish she couldn't help but smile. God had made that man strong, fast and determined. A protector.

Something in her periphery caught her eye. Two boats approached fast. She banged on the window and zoomed the binoculars. Two of the boats had big letters on the side. It was hard to tell what it said as the boats crashed through the waves, but she saw the first three letters of *Sheriff* so she flashed a thumbs-up at Kurt.

If his plan had worked, then the men who wanted her dead would follow shortly after them. Kurt opened the back door of the cabin and strode inside. He picked up a second set of binoculars and looked for himself. "They'll be up here in minutes."

"What if you misjudged how bad these private military guys want me gone, and they don't come?"

He put an arm around her shoulder, gave a small squeeze and stepped back as if he hadn't meant to do that. "It's driving me crazy that anyone would ever want to hurt you, so I'd be relieved. But, I also want to be prepared. The truth is that you've seen the flash drive numbers so your testimony could link the guard…and likely Mr. Cabell to murder. You can also identify Cabell as Mijovic. They don't know you still have a photograph, so…"

"So it's unlikely they'll let it go," she finished for him. She shrugged. "A girl can dream. It only looks like one person is driving each boat. What happened to your task force?"

He smiled. "Well, I don't envy any of them, particularly your grandfather, but they're hiding on the boat. I wanted to draw attention, but I also wanted to make it look like it would be an easy fight with only a few men. They probably think you and I are on one of those boats." He held up the binoculars. "I can see Delaney, and she's wearing plain clothes. If I didn't know better, she could pass as you from afar. She's put her hair in a loose braid—something I've never seen her do—because you do that."

She self-consciously fingered her braid. In the humidity, her hair got curlier. Delaney's had body and wave but her hair would braid so much easier than Rebecca's.

"Hopefully our plan works," he said. "We wouldn't want them to think they need to come here with guns blazing to overtake us. This will be all over fast enough." It might've been her imagination, but his eyes looked sad. He cleared his throat. "Okay, well they're pulling into dock. It's time to get you situated."

He turned to one of the many cabinets and unlocked it to reveal vests that looked more substantial than the one she had worn in the boat. He approached and held it for her to slip on like a coat. "This one has impact-resistance plate. I imagine they already have one on your grandfather."

"I'm sure he loves that."

He chuckled at her sarcasm. "They're not the most comfortable things on the planet." He tugged the straps, tightening it around her torso.

"I'm thinking of quitting." She blinked, surprised at herself, but it was true.

He straightened. "What do you mean?"

"My job. I think… I think I'm falling in love with the town." Her chest seized. What had just come out of her mouth?

"Really?" He took the smallest step closer to her and she didn't move away.

The air seemed to have left the cabin. No one breathed and only the sound of a bird in the distance could be heard. "Really," she whispered.

His eyes lit up. "It seems to me the town is already in love with you."

Her heart stopped for half a second. Did he really mean the town? Was he saying what she thought—

The back door slammed open. Delaney stood on the threshold with Rebecca's grandfather right behind her. "Believe it or not, the rails still work."

Her grandfather said nothing. His disapproving glare at the small space between Rebecca and Kurt said it all.

Kurt took an exaggerated step backward. "The team is bringing up our tactical gear?"

"Yes. They're setting up a perimeter before they enter, just in case we have visitors before dark." Delaney held out a bag. "And I picked up enough food from the office to take care of dinner." Poking out of the bag were dozens of the same emergency food packets that lined the cupboard. Rebecca's stomach didn't even dignify the dried food with a growl. Kurt fought a smile and offered an apologetic shrug.

Now that she had a better look, her grandfather appeared to have aged years since she'd seen him a few days ago. She crossed the wooden boards with her arms outstretched.

Grandpa pulled her close. Their vests bumping into each other made for an uncomfortable hug. "Are you okay?" She didn't miss the scathing look he sent Kurt.

"I'm fine, Grandpa. I'm more worried about you. How are you holding up?"

"Too much drama for my taste but otherwise I'm fine."

"You should've stayed in town."

"It's my fault you're in danger. They need to protect us both anyway so they can do it while we're together."

"It's going to be dark soon," Kurt said. "I think it's time to give you and Justice Linn the tour."

She reared back. "There's more to see?"

Kurt winked. Grandpa harrumphed.

"That's exactly why this is the safest choice," Kurt said. "Come on." He entered one of the side rooms that housed a couple of cots and a metallic bunk bed. He approached the closet, stepped inside and pressed the right side of it as he slid his hand sideways. It gave way and proved to be a pocket door that revealed a few stairs.

He flipped on the light, and she let him take care of a few spiderwebs before descending behind. Grandpa and Delaney lined up behind her. After the steps, the room opened up. It was essentially a giant basement, except it looked more like a modern house than the upstairs. She gaped. "Upstairs is a decoy?"

The walls were drywall, painted a light beige. There was a small kitchenette, complete with stove top and real kitchen cabinets that didn't look like they'd been there since the dawn of time. The coffee-colored couch and recliner needed a good dusting, but they would be comfortable down here. It was well lit, with additional lamps on the end tables. Delaney held up a handheld vacuum and took care of a couch cushion before offering it to Grandpa.

On the far end, a side room had two actual twin beds, not cots or metallic bedframes like the ones upstairs.

Kurt guided her to the far corner and pointed to a door with a dead bolt. "There's a second emergency exit here. No doorknob outside." He gestured to what looked like a closet door. "Bathroom here, but if for some reason we're still here tomorrow morning, I don't recommend using the shower until it's warmer. Solar-powered. And the water isn't drinkable."

Delaney approached the minifridge and plugged it in. "Speaking of water, I don't know about you, but I prefer cold water." She opened it to prove it was stocked with water bottles.

"So we wait down here while you catch these men?" Grandpa's voice came across as more of a bark.

"Yes, sir. Patton will be your guard down here. We'll be in constant contact. SWAT will cover the perimeter of the property." He glanced at the watch on his wrist. "Sunset should be happening right now. We're expecting the contracted mercenaries will attempt something tonight. We are equipped with infrared goggles. We'll see them coming. There's nothing to worry about." He gestured toward Delaney's bag. "When I give her the signal, we will go completely dark."

"Why? We don't have windows down here," Grandpa said.

"To prevent any chance they can discover this area down here, but she has infrared goggles for you to use, as well, if that would ease your mind." Kurt looked directly at Rebecca. "Hopefully the next time you see me the threat will be gone and you can move on with your lives."

Grandpa put his arms over his chest and Kurt disappeared through the fake closet. Delaney rubbed her hands together. "I'll make us some grub. I've never had these, but they have to be better than TV dinner, right?"

Rebecca shared a concerned glance with Grandpa. She imagined the packets could be worse, much worse.

"It's my fault," Grandpa muttered. "I'm an old man. I should've known."

"Grandpa, it's not your fault. Imagine if you hadn't asked for an audit, you might've been swindled and ruined your reputation."

"I'm not talking about that. I'm talking about the way you two look at each other. Forbidden love only fans the flame."

She tried not to roll her eyes at him but couldn't help it. "You think you can claim credit for me falling in love with him?"

Delaney dropped the pile of pots she'd been wrestling with a clank. Rebecca put a hand over her mouth and tried to avoid meeting Grandpa's wide eyes. Her heart had betrayed her aloud twice in the last hour. There seemed to be no denying it. She loved that man.

Each minute seemed like an hour. The men were all in position. Everyone watching. He'd moved the counter away from the wall so the three men, including him, could get closer to the wall facing the lake. Everything in the cabin was made with tactical situations in mind, so the cabinets and the counter were all detachable. The windows were bullet resistant but also pushed outward so they could take a shot, if needed. The plan was to take down the men without force, if possible.

There were plenty of private military soldiers who went on to lead productive lives, but the FBI had brought dossiers on the mercenaries who'd been tracked to the area. The men who would come tonight likely wouldn't lay down their weapons without a fight.

He shifted in the metal chair next to the window. The officers in the task force may have been from different branches, but they were all law enforcement and used to long waits. The marshal from Spokane sat next to the southern window and recounted the time he waited for a fugitive for eight hours in a closet just so he could get him without risk of injuring anyone else.

Similar stories came to mind and he could've participated in the camaraderie, but Kurt didn't have the heart to share. He wanted this to be over, to ask Rebecca to tell him more about what she had in mind for the future. Was it possible she'd meant she was falling for him instead of the town?

He knew what his words had meant, and the hollow feeling in his chest seemed to taunt him that he was vulnerable, not knowing where she stood. Her grandfather's demeanor had made it clear what he'd thought. Kurt's neck tensed, imagining the lecture Rebecca was likely receiving, with Delaney as an audience for good measure.

"Another message from headquarters," the FBI agent next to him muttered as he put away the satellite phone he'd brought. "Jorgenson keeps calling me. He's very anxious. He wanted to make this arrest himself. I think he's hoping no one shows up until tomorrow when he can be here."

"I don't think we have enough instant coffee for that scenario," Kurt replied.

He chuckled. "You know if you bag this guy, you're probably looking at a promotion, don't you?"

Kurt smiled. "I like the way you think, but we're after the guy Mijovic hired, not Mijovic himself."

"Yeah, but he'll lead you right to him."

"I don't like to count my chickens before—"

"Officially dark. IR goggles on," Fowley, the SWAT officer on the west side, ordered. He had the most experience with tactical stakeouts such as this one, so Kurt had asked him to be his point man. Fowley and the rest of the SWAT team each had a helmet that was already attached to his radio communications.

Kurt swiveled down his night-vision goggles from his helmet and slipped on the headphones designed to muffle the sound of gunfire. They also served as his radio communications, complete with microphone. Another gift the SWAT team had brought for everyone on the team. He addressed Delaney. "Patton, we're going dark."

"Affirmative."

A tense silence followed as everyone adjusted to the goggles. The trees in the distance came into focus. The greenish hue seemed fitting for the evergreens. He couldn't make a visual on the perimeter officer at the dock, though. "Newton, report."

Newton was the only one on the team with a high-powered thermal scope on his weapon. One of the SWAT officers on his left had a handheld thermal device, something they'd borrowed from the city's fire station, but Newton would likely spot any approach first.

Diagonal streaks of light hampered Kurt's distance vision.

The Spokane deputy marshal stomped his foot. "You've got to be kidding me! Since when was rain in the forecast?" Rain appeared as streaks with the infrared.

"Intermittent. Shouldn't last long," the SWAT officer answered. "Just remember that you'll be able to tell if anything is coming despite the interference as long as you don't see gaps in the background images."

Many of the men grumbled, and Kurt held back a groan. Rain interfered with thermal imaging, as well, but it didn't keep it from working. It just meant they had to look harder to really understand what they were seeing. He hoped Newton was up for the task, but he'd yet to report, maybe because he was fighting with his instruments in the sudden downpour. He clicked his earpiece. "Newton. Status."

Silence.

His spine tingled. He should have at least answered.

"Dalton. Status." Dalton was their second perimeter officer.

The crackling of static spiked his adrenaline. He couldn't see anything but someone should have answered. "Weapons up," Kurt said.

"Schmitt, here. Permission to leave post?"

"Permission granted."

"I thought I saw…it's what I didn't see. Part of the tree missing," the officer next to him said.

He should've known with an armored Hummer, these mercenaries didn't have the budget restrictions his men did. There was a possibility they were wearing infrared-resistant camouflage. If part of the tree was missing that likely meant a man was standing there. "Prepare to engage. Form outer perimeter and inner perimeter within these walls." Everything was going wrong. He could feel it in his gut. His plan had failed before it'd even started, and he wasn't going to let Rebecca pay the price for his failure.

Everyone in the cabin seemed to hold their breath as they waited. "Schmitt reporting. Dalton is down," the agent's voice whispered on the radio. "Taser probes on his legs and arms, and a syringe sticking out of his neck. But he's breathing."

"Tranquilizer," Fowley muttered. "It's likely what they did to Newton."

So they were taking his men out one by one, but at least they weren't killing them. Not yet.

Kurt slipped past the quick-moving men and spoke to Fowley directly. "Take the lead. Patton and I will bring the packages to swim, then I'll return alone."

"Affirmative." He nodded and then held up his weapon.

The men moved seamlessly, as if one unit, like they'd always been a team. The detective from the Sheriff's Office readied his rifle at the door. "Of course some arrogant politician in the seventies just had to go and name this place Ambush Alcove. We're supposed to be the ones who ambush—"

The front door exploded in a thousand pieces.

Kurt heard a foreign voice shout something he guessed meant "fire in the hole." He didn't wait for the fallout. He ran into the side room as he heard the boom. The mercenaries had likely thrown a flash bang diversionary device, highly effective for those not prepared for it. If he'd been without his ear protection, even without seeing the green flash while wearing his goggles, the bang would've made his insides feel like jelly, and he would've been too disoriented to move, let alone think.

He heard the men shouting orders at each other over the radio. Kurt shoved his microphone upward and remained silent. If Newton and Dalton had been compromised, it was possible someone would overhear any orders he made to Patton. He entered the closet, stepped inside the false door, closed it and shoved down the emergency lock bar behind him. No one else would be able to use that entrance now.

He heard the ammunition click in Patton's firearm. The downside of avoiding radio usage meant Patton was ready to shoot to kill. "Delaney, it's Brock." He dropped his weapon so it hung from his neck and held up his hands.

She didn't miss a beat. "What's the plan?"

He turned his face so he could see the room, and since he still had his goggles on, saw her greenish form drop the rifle.

"Stay offline for the moment," he said, "and don't lower your weapon."

The judge and Rebecca held hands on the couch. Both were wearing goggles and their impact-resistant ballistic vests.

"Things went south," he said. "We need to get you out of here." If there'd been any time, he'd reevaluate all the decisions that had led up to this moment. The bottom line was that he'd genuinely thought this would be the safest and most effective plan. Even if it wasn't, he couldn't waste any energy with second guesses.

"Delaney, you still wearing a braid?"

"No, but I'm on it now."

He opened one of the cabinets. "Rebecca, I need you and your grandfather to wear tactical gear."

"But I don't know how—"

"I don't want you to use it. Just look the part."

Delaney slipped off her belt. "She can use mine. It's already adjusted. It's a good plan, sir."

"Well, I don't know the plan." The judge's voice rose.

"They're tranquilizing our men. I imagine their orders have them only taking out—"

"Me," Rebecca said. "No. These are contracted killers. Delaney can't pretend to be me. I'm not taking your belt!"

THIRTEEN

Rebecca's stomach threatened to revolt against the wild rice soup she'd made herself eat an hour ago. It was hard enough to sit waiting while men put their lives on the line to stop the mercenaries, but she couldn't ask Delaney to take her place.

"If they go after me, I'll be ready," Delaney said. She approached Rebecca and wrapped the belt around her waist without asking. She gave the belt a hard pull and snapped it before Rebecca could react.

"I won't be unarmed," Delaney said. "We're a team. They've got my back. This is my job."

"No time for arguments. I wanted to be out by now." Kurt handed Rebecca a ball cap with the US Marshals logo. Their hands met and she wanted to see his eyes again, but all she could see were the circle shapes of the goggles over his eyes. "I'm hoping it won't even be an issue. Your safety is my highest priority." Her heart raced and while she knew it was his job to think like that, his words seemed to hold personal meaning. Her imagination had set her up for disappointment in the past, though.

Delaney handed her a jacket with US Marshals written on each sleeve.

She turned to find Grandpa wearing a similar hat and jacket. Through the goggles she finally understood why Kurt insisted. By looking at her Grandpa, she couldn't tell his age. He wore the uniform and the equipment and looked like a solider.

Kurt ran into the room with the beds and returned with blankets, which he flung at them. They must have been made of wool. She'd always hated the itchy fabric.

"Drape them over yourself."

She followed his instructions. "Can I ask why?"

"They're thick and if someone has obtained Newton's thermal scope, or worse, the mercenaries have their own thermal imaging, then the wool blankets will help defeat it." He spoke so fast she had to replay the words in her head to understand his point.

For an older man, Grandpa proved he could still move with agility. He swung the blanket over his jacket until it looked like a hooded cloak. She followed his example.

Kurt pulled down his communication microphone but only listened for a bit before flipping it up. "Okay, the men are engaged. Now's the time. Patton, you will escort them to the tram. I'll run down ahead of the rails to ensure safe passage to the dock. Get them to the boat and go. I'll assist SWAT. As soon as you're in range in Coeur d'Alene, request assistance from police."

"Understood, sir." Delaney positioned herself in front of Rebecca.

He strode to the back door and his hand hovered over the dead bolt. "If you see anything odd with your night vision, let me know immediately. No matter how insignificant."

Rebecca nodded out of habit, but no one was looking at her. The weight of the blanket, the jacket, the hat, the ballistic vest, and the tactical belt made her lungs and back hurt instantly. It had to take a tremendous amount of training and strength to ever get used to it.

Kurt's fingers flipped the dead bolt, but he hesitated. She knew once he went out the door, there was no coming back. He'd told her it was a one-way exit.

"Judging by the commands through comms, our men aren't overtaking the mercenaries. So far it's evenly matched, but if we stay here, they'd be sitting ducks." Delaney must have sensed his hesitation since her words seemed to be a response.

Kurt nodded. "Let's go."

Delaney held her rifle with two hands but stayed in front of the judge and Rebecca. Kurt scanned the area. The rain had eased up, but the wind had kicked in. The breeze blew back the makeshift hood Rebecca had donned. The green trees shifted; the branches in their eerie glow seemed to be waving at her. It was hard to believe she could see better with the goggles than if she yanked them off. As it was, the weird hue gave her the creeps, as if eyes were everywhere, watching her. An oval black hole sidled into her peripheral vision. She tilted her head, wondering if she'd imagined it. The fuzzy blackness moved. She pointed over Kurt's shoulder. "Black hole in that tree."

"Interference," Delaney yelled.

"Get down!" Kurt swung his rifle up to his shoulder.

His men would've shown up on the night goggles, which meant the blackness was one of the mercenaries. Kurt spotted the black hole, aimed for the center of it and squeezed the trigger. A bright light flashed and an intense force shoved into his chest. He staggered backward and momentarily lost his breath. He swept the area with the goggles to see if he'd made contact, as well. Delaney hadn't wasted a second. He could see her running with two shady gray objects, so he needed to make sure the focus remained on him.

He forced his legs to move forward while scanning the trees in front of him. The black hole moved, albeit more slowly this time. He didn't take the time to find his mark with the rifle again. Instead he lifted the handgun from his holster and shot it right into the middle of the darkness.

Branches snapped. Kurt sucked in a breath, past the pain in his ribs, and ran toward the direction of the shot. Hard metal swiped his leg and he fell onto the bumpy ground. A figure held a metal baton in his hands. The man ripped the helmet from Kurt's head.

Without the night vision, he felt blind for a half second too many as he waited for his eyes to adjust. The man dropped to a knee on his chest and the pressure was almost enough to make him pass out. His ribs, likely bruised from the vest taking the bullet, pressed against his burning lungs. "No more radio. Your friends can't help now." The thick accent was as Rebecca described, but Kurt had no way of knowing if it was the guard who'd first attacked her. All of the contracted soldiers could've originated from the same locale. The probability seemed high.

The guy shoved a giant hand over Kurt's neck, his thumb pushing into Kurt's windpipe. Kurt wheezed. His throat felt like it might collapse. The man pulled a gun from his belt and shoved it into Kurt's forehead. "Where'd you hide the girl? You might live if you tell me."

A hard, round rock poked into Kurt's side. His fingers wrapped around it. If it were smoother, it'd be the same size as a baseball. He reared back his arm as far over his head as the terrain allowed and let the rock fly into the man's face.

The soldier howled. Kurt braced one of the man's ankles with his leg and used his knee to vault the man off his torso. His throat burned so badly he saw spots. He couldn't afford to take even a second to recover.

Kurt popped up and shoved a knee into the man's lower back. His hands and arms worked as if on autopilot from years of practice. Within seconds, the guy's wrists were locked with an industrial-size yellow zip tie Kurt kept in his tactical belt. For good measure, Kurt wrapped another one around the guy's ankles. It wasn't standard operating procedure, but these men weren't standard, either.

Kurt stood on shaky legs. The rain soaked his hair and dripped down his face. He hunted until he could find his communication unit. "Patton?" he rasped.

"Secure," a deep voice that sounded like Fowley's answered. "We have four men. Minor injuries."

"Need assistance." Kurt tried to say it loud and clear, but his voice sounded like a croak.

It only took twenty seconds for a soldier he recognized to jog toward him to relieve him of holding the guy. But it was twenty seconds too long.

"Patton, status?"

The silence almost brought him back down to his knees.

* * *

Rebecca shivered, despite the thick blanket she held up over both her and Grandpa. Given everything she wore, she doubted it was the temperature or the weather that chilled her. The gunshots played on a repeating echo inside her mind. She was just as sure that one of the sounds had come from the woods as she was that one had come from Kurt's gun.

If Delaney hadn't dragged her by the wrist toward the side of the building, Rebecca wouldn't have been able to leave him alone. Her eyes burned, but she couldn't afford to cry. There was no fast way to wipe tears away inside the goggles.

Kurt could be dead by now. Her body shook harder until her teeth chattered. Grandpa sat next to her on the steel bench inside the carriage that would take them down the rails. It had a ledge to step on and off and raised walls on either side, but no roof. Delaney had left her with a handgun to slide down the steep hill ahead of them. But how would they have any idea if Delaney had made it down the passage safely or not? They hadn't discussed how many minutes to wait before she should press Go on the rail system. She had finally turned over a new leaf to become a planner, and none of it worked. Kurt's words seemed to echo in her mind. *The point is to be sensitive to what the Lord has in store for you.*

Okay, fine. She prayed silently with her eyes open, searching the trees around them for more black holes. *Lord, please keep Kurt safe.* She inhaled through her nose to push the pesky tears back. *I've finally reached the point where I'm convinced You have good things in store for me. I've seen Your hand in my life, and I'm*

*asking You to help me make the right decisions right
this minute. I know You sometimes use a still, small
voice and all, but please, in this instance, I'm asking
that You yell so I can hear over all this fear I'm trying
not to have.* Her fingers tensed around the handgun.

Grandpa had kept his blanket wrapped around him
like a cloak, but Rebecca didn't want to risk anyone
with night vision being able to see their faces. She
ripped off the infrared goggles and placed the gun on
her lap. She held the wool fabric up like a tent over
them. The wind shook the edges but the weight of it
wouldn't budge from covering their heads.

The blanket prevented her from scanning the
area, but even if she spotted another black hole, she
would never be able to aim and fire as Kurt had done.
She'd be too scared that the black oval was actually a
friendly. And there hadn't been time to ask clarifying
questions on whether or not Kurt or Delaney would
appear like black holes in trees, as well. She didn't understand how the things worked, so the safer option
seemed to be to stay hidden.

Back at the cabin, Delaney had said they were sitting ducks. That was the last thing Rebecca wanted,
and it'd been five minutes since she'd last seen Delaney, so she pressed the green button inside the
wooden lift. It jerked slightly before smoothly moving down the rail.

It hummed to life. The hum had to draw attention.
"Shh," she whispered without thinking.

Grandpa's chest shook slightly, but he didn't say
anything. Either he was laughing at her and wondering who she was trying to hush, or he was distraught
again. He'd been on an endless roller-coaster loop of

emotions ever since her admission about Kurt. According to him, if she really had fallen in love with Kurt, it would be the forever end to Grandpa's relationship with her father.

"He'll never speak to me again," he'd said. He'd followed up by claiming the entire mess was his fault because he was the reason she was in town in the first place.

The wind howled and the rain picked up, pattering against the wooden bucket they sat within. The boat she'd found so uncomfortable on the way to the cabin would now be a welcome haven, but she didn't want to leave without Kurt. The gun resting in her lap slid off her knees and hit the small space on the bench between them since both of her arms were busy holding up the blanket. Every second she counted in her head seemed like a minute because a barrage of questions interrupted each one. *Where was Kurt? Where was Delaney? Were the men captured?*

The blanket tugged and ripped from her fingers. The clouds shifted and the moonlight illuminated the security guard who'd attacked her. He flung the blanket he'd yanked off her to the side. He wore black goggles, so she couldn't see his cold eyes, but she'd recognize his leer anywhere. He leaned over the edge of the lift. "I knew I'd find you again." The man lifted his weapon toward her forehead. Images of herself and Grandpa in the dirt, bleeding, faces lifeless, bombarded her mind. She did the only thing that came to mind. She slapped the emergency stop button next to her hip.

The carriage jolted to a stop and the man lost his footing on the ledge outside the door and toppled backward. He caught himself with one hand on an ever-green branch. The gun remained in his right hand as he lifted his arm and aimed at her chest.

A small click sounded behind her. Grandpa had abandoned his blanket and stood tall. He pointed the handgun squarely at the guard. "Get away from my granddaughter." His voice had such power and surety Rebecca knew in an instant why criminals feared him.

"You heard the man," a hoarse voice announced to her left. "Drop it."

Rebecca craned her neck. Kurt held a wide stance on the steep terrain, but his legs seemed shaky. With two hands, he trained a weapon of his own on the guard. Water poured down her face in streaks, but Kurt didn't so much as blink even though the rain pelted him. The confidence on his face made her wonder if he'd trained in the rain, countless times, until he never missed.

The guard's hand twitched.

"Don't even think about it!" Ten feet directly below the guard, Delaney stood. "Put the weapon down now." She had a rip in her jacket and a trail of something dark, like blood, ran down the side of her face. She aimed her weapon at the back of the guard's head.

The guard scowled, but the weapon fell from his hand. Delaney and Kurt moved in unison. They launched themselves at the guard, pulling his arms behind his back and shoving his face against the ground. Kurt secured his arms and legs with a bright yellow plastic strap while Delaney flung the man's weapons far away from his person. They flipped him over and worked together to remove the arsenal from the man's vest and belt.

Kurt looked up briefly as Delaney recited the man's rights.

"Sir, you can lower the weapon now."

It took her a second to realize Kurt was talking to the judge. Grandpa exhaled and dropped the gun to the bench. His hands trembled as he pulled her into a hug. She sucked in a giant breath and let the tears roll down her face. The rain had lessened to a light mist but helped wash the strained emotions away. It was over.

If she ever questioned that God had her best interests at heart, she would always remember that not only one but three people had appeared to defend her. She wiped the tears away. Grandpa lifted her chin to see her face. The Marshals cap and the goggles were no longer on his head. The moonlight emphasized his tired eyes. "Are you okay, sweetie?"

"Yes." The immediate danger was over, but in the back of her mind she knew the man who wanted her dead was still out there. How many others would he hire to make sure she was dead? While she trusted the Marshals, a life in witness protection was the last thing she wanted. Her family's approval and love was everything to her and to be without it…

Movement from behind the windows in the cabin made her muscles tense. One window opened. "Turn your comms back on," a man shouted.

Kurt flipped his microphone down. "Brock reporting. Anyone hurt?" Kurt listened, and even though Rebecca couldn't hear what was being said she saw the relief on his face. "Good."

"I found Newton," Delaney said. "He'd been shot with what appears to be a tranquilizer."

"Let's hope it's nothing else," Kurt answered.

"He's breathing."

"We didn't want to kill anyone else," the guard said. "We only do what's contracted. Nothing more."

"Who did the contracting?" Delaney asked.

Kurt held his hand to his ear. "What? Seriously?" He narrowed his gaze at the guard. He pulled on the lip of his vest until the man was in a seated position. "Your men are trying to claim they were contracted by the US government to make a hit on Miss Linn."

"That is what they believe. Nothing is their fault. You must let them go."

Kurt put his fists on his belt. "There's nothing I must do except put you in jail. I can believe you might've told them the government ordered this, but we both know that wasn't true. So why would I help you go along with that?"

"Because I can hand you the boss who gave the orders. I have the flash drive the lady is missing plus more. Much more. I want to talk for a deal."

Hope sparked in Rebecca. The man was ready to give up the evidence and Cabell—Mijovic—whatever his name was… Maybe the nightmare really was about to end.

Delaney crossed her arms. "Do you know where Mijovic is now?"

"He hasn't left the area. I hid him well. I told him it was safest, but I wanted him close for insurance."

Kurt shook his head. "You were watching your back all along?"

"Men who hire us cannot always be trusted. You must know this."

"Here's a tip. Stop telling us what we *must* do. We'll

leave the deal making to the FBI," Kurt said. "They're taking over this case."

The third officer who wore an FBI jacket approached and grabbed the man's wrists. "My boss is in the air as we speak. He's looking forward to talking to you." He looked over his shoulder at Kurt. "We're taking the suspects on the sheriff boats."

"Coast Guard is on the way, Brock," Delaney said. "We can get a ride with them."

"Coast Guard?" the judge asked, his tone incredulous.

"They send someone to patrol about once a week in the spring and early summer, given all the party cruises and the size of our lake," Delaney explained. "We notified them we might need their services, and they came down early."

The judge exhaled. "I hope their boat is more comfortable than the one up here."

"I don't know about that, but I can promise you don't have to lie down under life vests this time."

Rebecca gaped. "Grandpa, you must be so sore."

The judge patted her arm. "I'm safe. You're safe. That's what matters. I think I'd like to get out of this rain while we wait."

Delaney climbed the hill to the other side of the carriage and helped Grandpa out. "I'll get you back inside, sir." On closer inspection, the line down the side of her face was mud.

Kurt swiveled the rifle hanging from his neck to the back of his chest. He put his helmet under the crook of his left arm and reached with his other hand for Rebecca. "Are you okay?"

She accepted his strong grip and climbed out of

FOURTEEN

"We'll be right there," Kurt answered. He was going to get a reputation at this rate.

Delaney held up a hand. "It's obvious you're debriefing." Even in the dim lighting, Kurt could see her wink. "I'm guessing we have a good ten minutes before our ride is here if you have anything else to... discuss. I'll let the judge know you'll be along shortly."

Rebecca turned back to Kurt, her face creased with worry. She didn't need to say it. He could see it on her face.

"Your family—"

She nodded and blinked hard. "But you saved my life," she said.

For a brief moment he wanted to take the credit, all the credit. "I think the judge actually did. He had a gun aimed before I got there, and even though I was there a second later, if he hadn't—" Kurt gulped. "I might've lost you. I have to make split-second decisions in this job. I try to make the best ones, but I'm not sure I made the right one tonight." He fought to find the right words, to do the right thing. "I don't want to come between you and your family, Rebecca. I don't want to cause anyone pain."

Her eyes searched his. "And I don't want to cause problems with your job."

His mind searched for another option, something out of the box that could fix it all, but he came up with squat. "So I guess it's for the best if we...if we forget what happened."

Her eyes widened and she put a hand on her neck. "Forget? The time with you won't be something I'll be able to forget." She stepped backward. A sad laugh left her lips. "Goodbyes are hard."

He tried to pull her close for a hug, but their vests made it a challenge. A spotlight washed across the lake and rested on the sheriff boat that was pulling away from the dock. From a loudspeaker, a man's voice announced the approach of the Coast Guard boat.

"Grandpa doesn't want to ride this tram again, but I imagine his knees would prefer it to the rope bridge." She offered a small smile, stepped inside the carriage and pressed a button that moved it upward toward the back of the cabin.

Kurt exhaled and his ribs hurt from the effort. His part in the investigation was almost done. The FBI would be taking over. Since the guard knew exactly where Mijovic was, assuming he was telling the truth, they would make a deal and apprehend the guy.

Now all that was left was to tell Rebecca goodbye.

One of the SWAT members approached. "The different agencies don't always work together so easily. Heard the Marshals' chief deputy for Idaho retired a while back and they haven't replaced him yet. You going for it?"

the lift. "I'm more worried about you. The gunshot I heard—" The trees blew gently in the breeze. The shadows moved and the moonlight hit the front of his vest. She gaped. "You've been shot!"

He dropped the helmet and put both hands on her shoulders. "I'm okay, Rebecca. The vest did its job. No doubt some bruises, but I'll be fine."

She searched his eyes for pain. Instead he only smiled down at her. She gulped down a new fear that cropped up. It wasn't the best time to talk, but if she didn't do it now, she'd lose her nerve. "Earlier... I didn't fully realize what I was saying, but I wanted to clarify. I wasn't talking about the town."

He released a deep chuckle that tickled her ears and warmed her heart. "I love you, Rebecca." He bent his head just enough to brush his lips over hers. He pulled back only an inch. "Is that enough clarification?" he whispered.

"I'm not sure." She smiled as his lips met hers again.

A feminine cough sounded behind them. Rebecca turned to find Delaney ten feet behind them. "The judge wanted to know what was keeping you."

Her face heated despite the breeze and her wet hair. "He was hurt—" She sucked in a deep breath. Why was that always the first excuse to fly out of her mouth?

A week ago he would've answered yes. Now he felt lost. "Not sure."

"Nice job leading a team." He slapped Kurt's back as he headed down the hill.

Kurt should've been pleased with the comment. Except the only team he wanted was a partnership with Rebecca.

The last two days had simultaneously moved at a snail's pace and been full. She'd decided to find a job as an accountant in Coeur d'Alene and stay with her grandpa. She'd spoken to her dad over the phone, and after he'd finished hyperventilating, he'd seemed to accept her decision. The past couple of nights had been in a hotel with Grandpa and Delaney. The last time she'd seen Kurt had been a wave from the Coast Guard boat.

"Good news," Delaney said. "We've had a hit on Mijovic's credit card. Las Vegas."

"Good. So you've located him?" Grandpa asked.

"It appears so. So we're lifting your protection detail. You can drive yourself around again and move back into your house, sir. Deputy Brock will stop by tonight to confirm your security system is working and your property is secure."

It might've been her imagination, but Rebecca thought Delaney had added a wink toward her. It didn't matter. She knew where she stood with Kurt. Getting her freedom back should've cheered her up, but instead she accepted Grandpa's car keys and ran errands. The entire time her mind and heart were in a fog. It might've been part of the reason that she ended up letting the vet talk her into bringing home two cats instead of one.

Grandpa's house still carried the aroma of smoke if you sniffed a couple of times, but he'd brought in professionals to clean all the furniture and carpet in the rest of the house that wasn't being replaced. New garage doors had been installed, and there were new windows, flooring and cabinets in the kitchen. The only thing lacking was paint on the new drywall in the dining area and a dining room table. Grandpa dragged his feet on that purchase until she realized Grandma had always picked out their furniture. It made Rebecca glad she'd decided to stay with him even more.

The doorbell rang and she stiffened. She'd debated about taking a walk to avoid seeing Kurt, but in the end, she didn't want to miss another chance to see him. Would he act friendly toward her or act like he used to when he was trying not to talk to her?

She stepped into the hallway as Grandpa and Kurt discussed the new security system. Kurt ran the system through diagnostic tests. "Okay, sir, it looks like you're all set."

She knew the moment he'd spotted her. His spine straightened and he smiled. "I hear you're still planning to move to Coeur d'Alene?"

Her shoulders dropped, thankful he wasn't avoiding her. "I've put in my notice, and I've actually started planning my move."

"You?"

She laughed. "Well, once you start, it kind of gets addicting. Plus, I got a cat."

"You got a cat?"

"I told Grandpa I'd pick up Queen B for him at the vet."

"Queen B?" Grandpa asked. "You got a third cat?" His voice raised an octave.

"No, that's what the vet calls Babette. Didn't Grandma ever tell you that? Anyway, they wanted to show me this other Siamese mix they'd recently acquired because the owner had passed. Apparently, while Babette was in boarding, they fell in love. I couldn't just leave him there."

The cat, as if knowing he was being discussed, entered the room and wove around her feet. She leaned down and stroked his fur. Finally a cat that seemed to enjoy her attention. "Meet Siameanie."

Kurt crossed his arms at his chest. "A kitty named Siameanie? With that name, I'd assume it's not the nicest."

"I'll rename him Si." Babette appeared and looped her way around Kurt's legs before flopping into the space between Kurt and Rebecca. Si flopped next to her, and the two cats pawed at each other playfully. "Apparently he used to be aggressive until Babette came along. The vet said he just needed a good woman."

"I know the feeling." His eyes widened as if he hadn't meant to say that aloud.

Her heart pounded. They stared at each other. She was momentarily at a loss for words. "Wh...what about you? You plan on going for that promotion?"

"I might actually request a transfer. It might...might be easier, all things considered."

Her gaze dropped to the ground. "Yes. Maybe."

"It's been an honor getting to know you, Rebecca. Take care, but..." He pulled in a deep breath. "Call me if you need anything." He frowned, nodded abruptly and walked out the door.

Her throat and chest seized, clenched by an unseen vise.

"So you're definitely moving to Coeur d'Alene? This isn't just a passing fancy?"

She'd forgotten Grandpa was in the room. So, he'd likely heard everything. "I was serious, Grandpa. Believe it or not, I've thought about it for years. The past few days have made it clear to me that it's a good choice."

"Even after everything you've gone through here?"

She picked up a photograph taken years ago when she was a child. Her entire family, her aunt, a smiling Grandma and Grandpa were in front of the lake. "Some of my best memories are here. I love this town." Her voice caught on the last word as she remembered what those words had meant when she'd said them to Kurt.

"Why didn't you go after him?"

She spun to find Grandpa frowning. "What do you mean?"

"You love him. Isn't the feeling mutual?"

"It's…it's complicated."

His shoulders dropped. "Time to time, I might forget that you're a grown, intelligent woman of God. But the Lord hasn't forgotten. His approval is all you really need, honey. I'll get used to whoever you end up with…and I imagine, with time, your dad will, too." He tilted his head and studied her face. "You remind me so much of your grandmother, you know. I'd be so happy if you decided to make a home here. And Kurt… Well, I suppose he's a good man, or I wouldn't have trusted him with your safety." He sighed. "It took me ten years to win over your grandmother's family. I'm sure Kurt can handle waiting that long." He winked.

"What?" Her mouth dropped. Her grandma had been so close to her own family Rebecca had never imagined that they hadn't adored the match. "They didn't like you?"

"They *hated* lawyers. All lawyers."

A wobbling laugh escaped her throat. "Oh, Grandpa." She rushed into his arms and hugged him.

"What are you waiting for? Go after him."

She didn't need to be told twice.

She spun around right into the barrel of a gun.

Kurt drove along the driveway and stopped when he reached the road. He clenched the steering wheel. Was it right to let her go like that? It seemed like he was doing the honorable thing. He was willing to deal with heartache if it meant a better, happier life for Rebecca. But was that really what was happening?

He let his head drop to the steering wheel. At this moment he didn't care whether or not he ever got a promotion. He did love his job, but if Rebecca asked him to do something else, he'd be willing. So if her family's approval was the only thing standing in the way, he was willing to do what he needed.

He'd talk to her grandfather and her father. He smiled at the thought. It might be his scariest assignment yet. Kurt pulled out his phone and prepared to text Rebecca to see if she could come outside for a private chat.

His phone had a slash through the tower. That was odd. He always had a good signal in the area. Something nagged at the back of his mind, but he couldn't really pinpoint it.

Kurt leaned over and retrieved the satellite phone from the back seat. No signal, either. His heart rate escalated. That was more than odd. To have both go out at the same time likely meant someone was using a jammer in the area.

When someone had first broken into the house, they'd overridden the alarm system. The guard had admitted during debriefing that Mijovic had supplied the equipment and know-how to do that. This new system had more bells and whistles, but the communication scenario was the same. It used a direct landline to contact the police. If that was cut or unavailable for some reason, it relied on a cellular backup.

Kurt pulled his weapon and jumped out of the truck. No sign of movement near the windows. He left the truck door open in case slamming the door would be heard from inside. He crept along the driveway until he reached the front door. If he was right, the door would open without an alarm. If he was jumping to conclusions, her grandfather would have another reason to disapprove of him.

He took a deep breath and prayed the hinges didn't creak as he pressed the lever and swung it open. No lock enabled and no alarm. Mijovic had to be here, but why would he come back? Rebecca wasn't the one testifying against him, wasn't the one holding the evidence. It was the guard. So what good did it do to return? Obviously the credit card hit in Las Vegas had to be a wild-goose chase.

Babette weaved around his legs. Kurt tried to rein

in his frustration. Really? Now? He took a step and the wooden floor creaked.

"What do you want?" Judge Linn asked from around the corner.

Kurt couldn't see the interchange but overhearing it was enough to confirm his suspicions.

"You," Mijovic replied. "Americans like their federal judges. They give them more protection than others. It's very simple. You will come with me until they unfreeze my accounts. Then you can board a plane and come back to your country."

"You want to take me somewhere with no extradition?" The judge laughed. "I don't think so."

"Think of it like a vacation."

Kurt tried to take another step and the floor creaked again. He cringed as Mijovic asked, "Is someone else here?"

Kurt used his foot to nudge the cat. Babette didn't appreciate it and ran off into the living room. Hopefully that would answer Mijovic's question. Kurt stepped diagonally in the hope he avoided the joist areas that creaked.

"Our government doesn't negotiate with terrorists," the judge said. "And even if you get your money and you get out of the States, that doesn't mean the US can't hunt you down."

Kurt recoiled. Was the judge trying to make Mijovic angry enough to shoot? He glided forward until he could see Mijovic around the wall.

The judge's face had grown red. "The CIA wouldn't hesitate to kidnap and forcefully bring a man like you—"

"What he's trying to say is we are no threat to you,"

Rebecca interjected. "You can walk out that door." She held up her hands, no doubt in an effort to calm both her grandfather and Mijovic.

"I'm pretty sure Americans do not like accountants." Mijovic waved his gun.

"No!" Judge Linn shouted. "I'll go with you. Leave her alone."

Kurt didn't need to hear any more. He took the remaining amount of space at a run.

Mijovic raised his weapon.

Kurt slid into him at full speed, crashing into his side and shoving his arm upward. He punched Mijovic in the chest and reached to grab his wrist. A gunshot rang out and glass rained from the ceiling light fixture. Kurt slipped his foot behind the man, twisted his torso and slammed his elbow into Mijovic's back, flipping him to the ground.

Kurt put a knee in his stomach and smashed the guy's wrist down onto the wooden floor until he released his hold on the weapon. He pointed his own weapon into the man's face, rage surging through his veins. It took self-control he didn't know he possessed to not pull the trigger. Mijovic had almost taken the life of the woman he loved. "You have the right to remain silent, and I highly recommend you use it." He rattled off the rest of Mijovic's rights.

"Now that is what I call a home run," the judge remarked. "Excellent timing. Rebecca tells me you used to be a baseball player. Any chance you might consider returning to the sport?"

"Grandpa," Rebecca groaned.

He chanced a look at Judge Linn to see a teasing

grin on his features. "You saved her life and most likely saved mine. Again. I suppose you're all right."

Rebecca beamed, her eyes misty. "You came back."

Kurt wanted to respond immediately, but he had a job to do first. He flipped the man over and secured his wrists. "I realized that I couldn't give you up without a fight. I love you."

He stood and Rebecca ran to him. "You've already won. I love you, too."

EPILOGUE

Rebecca rushed out of her job as city auditor exactly at five o'clock. She barely heard her coworkers shout out well wishes. It was Wednesday, which meant it was her standing weekday dinner date with Kurt when he was in town, but today butterflies flipped in her stomach. It was Valentine's Day. They'd known each other for almost a year. A glorious, wonderful, adventurous year.

Her boots slapped against the asphalt as she rushed around her car for a quick safety check. Some habits died hard, but this one didn't seem like one she had to give up. Fear didn't well up.

It took five minutes to drive home—she shared the house with Grandpa, an arrangement she'd feared would end up stifling, but so far had been beneficial to them both. The house was empty, though, which was odd. She didn't know of her grandpa having any plans for Valentine's, and he had scaled back to part-time hours with the courts. She placed a heart-shaped box of chocolates on the counter for him and rushed to change into a maroon dress. Her unruly curls finally submitted to a fresh round of spritzer as she pulled up the sides into a barrette.

Her phone buzzed.

Do you mind meeting me at the restaurant? I'm running late. Sorry.

She exhaled. His tone seemed more like a normal date than a special date. Right? So he probably wasn't going to propose. Logically there was no reason to get her hopes up, so she needed to calm down. She slipped on her fuzzy winter boots and hoped they didn't look too out of place with the dress.

Fat snowflakes descended from the gray, heavy clouds in the sky.

The Cedar Floating Restaurant was the most romantic restaurant in town. She pushed aside the self-consciousness and passed couples, staring into each other's eyes, on the boardwalk. The host inside seemed to recognize her even though she'd never been there. Either that, or she was the only single person here on the holiday. "Miss Linn? Your party is here."

The nerves rose to the surface. *Lord, help me be calm and not rush things. Your timing. Your plan.*

Kurt rose from his chair. He smiled and pulled her chair out for her. "Happy Valentine's Day." He kissed her cheek and sat in his own chair.

A peck on the cheek probably meant no proposal. She took a deep breath. Time to just enjoy a wonderful night.

He held up a shopping bag. "Before I forget, on my

last fugitive case, I came across this shop and thought you might like this."

Her trembling hands opened the bag to find a red glittery cat collar and a second cat collar with a red bowtie attached. Babette and Si would look so cute in them. "I knew you'd warm up to the cats. You love them."

She might've imagined it, but it looked like he blushed.

"So, this is kind of spontaneous..." he said.

"You're changing the subject."

"Because I have a question."

Oh, boy. She gulped, smiled and nodded. "Yes?"

"Would you like to join the co-ed softball team at church with me?"

She blinked rapidly and closed her gaping mouth. Softball. She fidgeted with the edges of the tablecloth. It was actually a great question. He hadn't enjoyed anything baseball related since his days in high school, even though it was obvious he loved the sport.

"I spoke to my dad," he said. "He might even be willing to travel here and do some guest coaching or refereeing one or two times."

That was also a huge deal. He'd reconnected with his father. She brushed off her initial disappointment and reached across the table to grab his hand. "I would love to be on a team with you."

Kurt looked over her shoulder then met her eyes. "True confession. Although, I'd been thinking about it, I wasn't planning to ask you that tonight. I was stalling."

"Stalling?"

He slipped off his chair to take a knee but didn't let go of her fingers. His hand shook around hers. "Please marry me."

Her heart rate went through the roof. "Y—"

"Wait. I think I should try that again." He pulled out a black box from his suit with his other hand and offered her a lopsided, gorgeous smile.

"Rebecca Linn, will you please do me the honor—"

"Yes!" She laughed aloud and jumped out of her chair. She sank down on her knees before he could get up, wrapped her arms around his neck and kissed him. His hands gripped her waist.

He lifted his head and grinned. "You haven't even looked at the ring."

"You're what matters." And she meant it.

"I needed to stall because someone wanted to be here for this." He didn't remove his hands from her waist, but he gestured with his chin to someone behind her. She turned her neck to see her parents and her grandpa watching them...as well as most of the restaurant attendees. Grandpa beamed and nodded his approval. Her mom and dad were both laughing and wiping tears from their eyes.

"You won them over. Grandpa's going to be jealous. It took him ten years to win over his in-laws."

"I'm just happy that it's the first time you've kissed me in public without me being injured."

She laughed and tilted her head. "It was worth the wait, wasn't it?"

He pulled her close. "Hmm, I forget. Remind me?"

"Happily." Rebecca's heart almost burst with the knowledge that her family approved of their plan to get married and, more importantly, her heavenly father did, as well. She leaned forward and soundly kissed him, at peace with their plans for the future, yet fully wanting to live in the moment.

This particular moment sent a spark all the way down to her toes.

* * * * *

Dear Reader,

Thank you for going on the adventure with me to Coeur d'Alene. If you ever have a chance, it's a gorgeous place to visit.

I enjoyed developing the romance between Rebecca and Kurt, as they are so different from any other characters I've written in the past.

Letters from readers are the best, and I invite you to contact me or sign up for my newsletter at writingheather.com.

Blessings,
Heather Woodhaven

COMING NEXT MONTH FROM
Love Inspired® Suspense

Available March 6, 2018

NIGHT STALKER
FBI: Special Crimes Unit • by Shirlee McCoy

After FBI special agent Adam Whitfield's ex-wife is nearly killed when she
stops an abduction, the serial killer Adam's been hunting turns his focus on
Charlotte Murray for getting in his way. Now Adam has two missions: bring
the murderer to justice...and save Charlotte.

GUARDING THE BABIES
The Baby Protectors • by Sandra Robbins

Back in her hometown to take custody of her recently orphaned niece
and nephew, country singer Holly Lee soon learns someone will go to any
lengths to kidnap the twins—even murder. And the only person she can trust
to protect them is her ex-boyfriend, Deputy Sheriff Cole Jackson.

TREACHEROUS TRAILS
Gold Country Cowboys • by Dana Mentink

When farrier Ella Cahill is accused of murder, only former marine
Owen Thorn—her brother's best friend—doesn't think she's guilty. But can
they work together to clear her name before she becomes the next to die?

THE LITTLEST TARGET
True North Heroes • by Maggie K. Black

On the run with a baby after witnessing her employer's murder, nanny
Daisy Hayward will protect the child with her life. And when paramedic
Max Henry comes to her rescue after her car is run off the road, he vows not
to let her or the little boy out of his sight until he's sure they're safe.

SECRET SERVICE SETUP
The Security Specialists • by Jessica R. Patch

Framed for corruption by an online mystery man, Secret Service agent
Evan Novak must prove he's innocent—and dodge the criminals who've
put out a hit on him. And his ex-girlfriend Jody Gallagher—a former
Secret Service agent turned private security specialist—is determined to
act as his bodyguard.

FUGITIVE SPY
by Jordyn Redwood

When Casper English is brought into the ER with amnesia, physician
Ashley Drager learns he has a picture of her in his pocket...and the same
tattoo as her long-missing father. Can she help him regain his memory—and
keep him alive—in time to find out what happened to her father?

**LOOK FOR THESE AND OTHER LOVE INSPIRED BOOKS WHEREVER
BOOKS ARE SOLD, INCLUDING MOST BOOKSTORES, SUPERMARKETS,
DISCOUNT STORES AND DRUGSTORES.**

LISCNM0218

Get 2 Free Books,

Plus 2 Free Gifts—

just for trying the Reader Service!

YES! Please send me 2 FREE Love Inspired® Suspense novels and my 2 FREE mystery gifts (gifts are worth about $10 retail). After receiving them, if I don't wish to receive any more books, I can return the shipping statement marked "cancel." If I don't cancel, I will receive 4 brand-new novels every month and be billed just $5.24 each for the regular-print edition or $5.74 each for the larger-print edition in the U.S., or $5.74 each for the regular-print edition or $6.24 each for the larger-print edition in Canada. That's a savings of at least 13% off the cover price. It's quite a bargain! Shipping and handling is just 50¢ per book in the U.S. and 75¢ per book in Canada*. I understand that accepting the 2 free books and gifts places me under no obligation to buy anything. I can always return a shipment and cancel at any time. The free books and gifts are mine to keep no matter what I decide.

Please check one: ☐ Love Inspired Suspense Regular-Print ☐ Love Inspired Suspense Larger-Print
(153/353 IDN GMWT) (107/307 IDN GMWT)

Name _____
(PLEASE PRINT)

Address _____ Apt. # _____

City _____ State/Prov. _____ Zip/Postal Code _____

Signature (if under 18, a parent or guardian must sign) _____

Mail to the **Reader Service**:
IN U.S.A.: P.O. Box 1341, Buffalo, NY 14240-8531
IN CANADA: P.O. Box 603, Fort Erie, Ontario L2A 5X3

Want to try two free books from another line?
Call 1-800-873-8635 or visit www.ReaderService.com.

* Terms and prices subject to change without notice. Prices do not include applicable taxes. Sales tax applicable in N.Y. Canadian residents will be charged applicable taxes. Offer not valid in Quebec. This offer is limited to one order per household. Books received may not be as shown. Not valid for current subscribers to Love Inspired Suspense books. All orders subject to approval. Credit or debit balances in a customer's account(s) may be offset by any other outstanding balance owed by or to the customer. Please allow 4 to 6 weeks for delivery. Offer available while quantities last.

Your Privacy—The Reader Service is committed to protecting your privacy. Our Privacy Policy is available online at www.ReaderService.com or upon request from the Reader Service.

We make a portion of our mailing list available to reputable third parties that offer products we believe may interest you. If you prefer that we not exchange your name with third parties, or if you wish to clarify or modify your communication preferences, please visit us at www.ReaderService.com/consumerschoice or write to us at Reader Service Preference Service, P.O. Box 9062, Buffalo, NY 14240-9062. Include your complete name and address.

LIS17R3

SPECIAL EXCERPT FROM

Love Inspired.
SUSPENSE

*After FBI special agent Adam Whitfield's ex-wife,
Charlotte Murray, is nearly killed when she stops
an abduction, the serial killer Adam's been hunting
turns his focus on her for getting in his way.
Now Adam has two missions: bring the murderer
to justice…and save Charlotte.*

*Read on for a sneak preview of **Shirlee McCoy**'s,
NIGHT STALKER, the exciting first book of the
miniseries **FBI: SPECIAL CRIMES UNIT**,
available March 2018 from Love Inspired Suspense!*

"Charlotte, I'm sure you know exactly why leaving the hospital isn't a good idea."

"The Night Stalker doesn't know who I am. He doesn't know where I live, and as far as law enforcement can tell, he left town and hasn't returned."

"Law enforcement has no idea who he is or where he lives."

"Wren said the Night Stalker probably hunted for his victims far away from home. If that's the case, he doesn't live anywhere near here," she commented.

"He changed his MO when he went after Bethany. He's always taken women from large hospitals. This time, it's different."

"That doesn't mean he lives close by."

"It doesn't mean that he doesn't," Adam pointed out.

"I don't know what you want me to say, Adam."

"I want you to say that you're going to follow the team's plan."

"What plan? The one where I get on a private jet and travel to an unknown destination?"

"Yes."

"Were you part of making it? Is that why you want me to agree to it?"

"You know I'm on leave," he said. "I have nothing to do with the plans that are made."

"I'm sure you'd like to be part of the decision-making process. You can go back to Boston and back to work," she replied, and felt like an ogre for it. Adam had been nothing but kind, and she'd done nothing but try to push him away.

"No. I can't. Not until I know you're safe."

"I don't need you to keep me safe," she murmured, but her heart wasn't in the words. They sounded hollow and sad and a little lonely.

"I didn't say you did. I said I need to know you are. I still care about you, Charlotte. That has never changed. For the record," he said, "I don't approve."

"Your disapproval is noted."

"But you're leaving anyway?"

"Yes."

"I'll get a wheelchair. I'll be right back."

Minutes later, he wheeled the chair in. "River and Wren are accompanying us to your place. They'll be staying there until you make a decision about protective custody."

"I don't remember agreeing to that."

"You didn't."

She could have argued.

She could have listed a dozen reasons why she didn't want or need federal officers in her house. Except that she wasn't 100 percent sure she didn't need them.

If the Night Stalker really did live somewhere nearby, he might be someone she knew, someone who'd recognized her.

Someone who wanted to make sure that she didn't recognize him.

Don't miss
NIGHT STALKER by Shirlee McCoy,
available March 2018 wherever
Love Inspired® Suspense books and ebooks are sold.

www.LoveInspired.com

Copyright © 2018 by Shirlee McCoy

Looking for inspiration in tales
of hope, faith and heartfelt romance?

Check out **Love Inspired**® and
Love Inspired® **Suspense** books!

New books available every month!

CONNECT WITH US AT:

Harlequin.com/Community

 Facebook.com/HarlequinBooks

Twitter.com/HarlequinBooks

Instagram.com/HarlequinBooks

 Pinterest.com/HarlequinBooks

ReaderService.com

Love Inspired®

LIGENRE2018

Reward the book lover in you!

Earn points from all your Harlequin book purchases from wherever you shop.

Turn your points into *FREE BOOKS* of your choice
OR
EXCLUSIVE GIFTS from your favorite authors or series.

Join for FREE today at
www.HarlequinMyRewards.com.

Harlequin My Rewards is a free program (no fees) without any commitments or obligations.

MYR17